Gulfside Wish

A HAVEN BEACH NOVEL

REBECCA REGNIER

One

JESSIE

She watched the little red button circle around and count down.

"Three, two, one. Hi, it's Jessie Jenkins! Gonna wait for a moment or two to start this Get Ready With Me, so a lot of you can hop on." It was 5:30 a.m.

Jessie looked at her phone, propped on a state-of-the-art tripod. A ring light illuminated her face. She had an array of products spread out before her, ready to apply meticulously. She glanced at her phone screen and watched the numbers rise—234, 320, 450 people on her livestream.

"I can answer a few questions before we start," she said brightly into the camera.

She read the comments and then picked up a hair clip. She squeezed the ends of a light-pink velvet-covered clip, gathered the front lock of her thick blonde hair, and then pinned it away from her forehead. Jessie's skin was smooth and shiny, almost like glass. Her mother said it looked greasy.

"I guess that's the style these days." She could hear her mother say.

It was the style; to achieve it, Jessie did endless laser peels, exfoliations, and derma-blading. Her aesthetician was a brand partnership deal, thank goodness. It was another thing Landon would freak out about. He had taken to calling her "superficial." It was a joke, really; he'd picked her when they were dating because she was "his little Barbie." And now, as she pushed forty, trying to keep that look, well, it cost money. The endless cycle of brand deals to pay for her treatments, so she could look good for the camera to do the brand deals.

Jessie looked at her phone again. Comments were scrolling by. That was good. Lately, things had slowed a bit on all her platforms. But this morning her followers were with her, and she worked hard to engage with as many as she could.

"You're so pretty!" Jessie said, reading a comment. She read it aloud to her growing livestream audience. "Oh, that's so nice," she replied.

"You don't even have to wear makeup," remarked another of her followers.

She laughed. "Oh, I do—you're about to see!"

Jessie gave each of her viewers a smile. She was genuinely happy to have her viewers and tried to never take them for granted.

She looked at the number again. There were now 2,000 people watching her live. It had been less than one minute.

She looked at the questions again. Bingo. This one was the one she'd hoped for. She'd read the question, talk about her outfit, and direct her followers to her online shop. It would appear organic to her followers. They'd think, "Oh, Jessie SWEARS by this sweater!"

That's what worked best. Appearing organic.

"Where did you get your sweater?" she said and then went on to explain.

"Oh, there's a link to this in my LTK shop! I love it—it's from Zara..."

Every brand she mentioned, every link she put up, was potential income.

Another question scrolled by.

"How do you keep your kids so quiet when you're doing this?"

"Oh, they're still asleep, thank goodness. You should've seen what I looked like at drop-off yesterday!" More relatability, organic, natural, but also smooth as glass. That was the balancing act Jessie performed daily.

It was true. She'd looked like crap yesterday. She hadn't got out of the car when she'd dropped the kids off to dance. She'd watched them go in—the last thing she needed was someone taking a picture of her without her extensions, without her makeup, without her branded tracksuit. She didn't mention any of that now, however. She just pretended they were all the same. Everyone could relate to looking less than glamorous at school pick-up and drop-off.

Jessie looked at the number again. There were now 5,000 people on her livestream. A couple of nasty comments came in. That was part of the deal. Some people came on her social media out of pure hate.

She took a moment and immediately blocked a couple of clearly disgusting weirdos. Trolls were fine—they upped engagement and put her livestream in front of new potential followers—but sickos? KTHNXBAI!

"Okay, we've got about 5,000 of us or so in here—a little smaller group for us. I think it's time to start, though. So, I promised you I would show you my no-makeup makeup routine."

She started with primer. Using her perfectly manicured nails, she tapped the expensive bottle with a clickity-click-click.

Jessie applied the product to her turned-up nose, high cheekbones, and chiseled jaw—all part of her online success: looks.

Her dad thought she should be a model when she was a kid, but at 5'3", modeling was out of the question. As a social media influencer, though, there was no height requirement.

Jessie proceeded to put no less than seven products on her face for her "no-makeup makeup look." She described each one, clicking her fingernails onto the jars, tubes, and potions she used. She made sure the camera had a good look at every label.

"Don't forget, every one of these products is in my store," she said.

At the end, she looked worthy of a red carpet, much less drop-off and pick-up at the kids' school. Comments were rolling in—questions: What was her favorite mascara? How did she keep from getting under-eye wrinkles? Where did her nail polish color come from?

She answered them all the same way: "Shoot me a DM and I'll send you all the links, easy peasy." She had an app that autoreplied to the DMs. Easy peasy.

After twenty minutes of applying her makeup, the "get ready with me" was about done. She could see the number of people start to drop off, an indicator that it was time to go. She needed to figure out how to keep viewers past twenty minutes; thirty minutes was her next goal. The real golden goose were livestreams that lasted over one hour. But she just hadn't hit on an idea worth one hour of viewer loyalty.

Loyalty, that reminded her, get those emails!

"Don't forget to subscribe! And, of course, jump into my DMs, and I'll send you a link to where I got this really great brush for applying foundation."

She saw 200 people in her DMs. Her affiliate links would go out to those followers. She hoped they bought something; good grief, she needed that to happen. Especially now, with Landon's stunt.

"Thanks, you guys, for watching. Don't forget—tomorrow we're picking out outfits for the girls for our photo shoot!"

Jessie gave her signature wink-and-wave sign-off.

She flipped off the livestream and took a deep breath. Her closet was the main stage for her "get ready with me" videos.

Jessie had started doing them during the pandemic and found, at first, it was just fun. She had her cosmetology license and a degree in fashion merchandising, so when it came to internet fashionistas and beauty experts, she did have credentials.

She never thought she'd be doing this for a living—but they were making money. Landon wasn't 100% in love with her career choice. He liked that she earned money, and at one point, she was out-earning him. He did well as the manager of the Ford Dealership, but in the heyday of her business, she doubled their income. His enjoyment of her success was short-lived. And now, her income very well may be a liability. She prayed it didn't come to that.

Still, the pressure was on her to keep it up. Her viewers expected her to have the trendiest home décor, the viral outfits, the big hair, and the smallest pores. She didn't want to disappoint them, because if she did, who knew if they'd come back?

She'd heard horror stories of influencers who stepped wrong, said the wrong thing, or made the wrong choice, and their careers were over. Worse than that, their lives were ruined.

Somehow, she'd put herself in a position that felt, on the one hand, empowering—because she was earning a living—and on the other, terrifying—because it could disappear with one wrong move.

Jessie carefully put all the products back in their specific places on her vanity. She changed clothes from her matching tracksuit to a Florida Gators T-shirt and a pair of jeans.

She needed to get the girls up, ready, and off to school. And then she'd have to clean the pantry. Tomorrow, she had scheduled a pantry tour for her followers, and she knew it had to look perfect.

Everything had to be perfect for the camera.

Even though nothing was perfect in her life.

Two

JOETTA

If you had asked Joetta Armstrong a few years ago if she would ever leave her husband, there was virtually no scenario she could imagine where her answer would be yes. But here she was.

Banks had listened to her story about her life with Bruce Kelly. He'd asked a question or two about her three daughters, but he'd mostly looked like someone who was shocked more than outraged. That was at first.

She knew she had borrowed this life, knew it. And now she had to give it back.

The previous decades with Banks had been her happily ever after.

Banks was never cross with her. He wanted more for her than she wanted for herself, and he had built a comfortable life for them —the life she had been raised to fit into.

It was all based on a lie. She had lied to him from the beginning; she had spent decades pushing the truth as far down in her memory as she could manage.

She had come clean to Banks. He'd listened. He was clearly shocked, but he still wasn't cross. He'd appeared to be patient with her, if not outwardly sympathetic to her. Maybe he'd get there. Digesting her lie would take time, much less accepting her again. She'd wait for Banks to come around. She owed him everything.

But somewhere along the line, Banks' shock had turned into something else. She hadn't expected him to get over the earth-shattering news. She never would. But it was as she had feared: Banks looked at her differently now, if he looked at her at all.

At first, there were still the day-to-day kindnesses that he had always bestowed upon their union. They had lived sweetly with each other, gently. And she knew how much he did care for her. Banks checked to make sure her car's oil was changed. He bolted the security locks on the house every night. He insisted she text him whenever she got where she was going when she was driving anywhere. She would send a heart emoji, and he'd send two back. They were very proud of themselves when they learned how to use emojis at their age! They were so hip. They laughed at themselves and their daughters sweetly teased them for their tech prowess.

It was a sweet life she'd built, an easy one, a soft one. But since she'd told Banks the truth, it was feeling tinny and hollow.

A day ago, Joetta had left the house to meet Blair at her latest OB appointment. It was across town. As was her habit, she texted Banks when she arrived. She sent her typical heart. And she waited.

There was no answer from Banks. No heart, no reminder to avoid I-75 where they've got that resurfacing project, or whatever little thing he wanted to protect her from. Banks thought of everything.

Joetta's relationship with Bruce had been so different. He'd expected her to be competent and tough. All the Kelly women were. She'd failed to live up to that standard by a mile.

As a result, she'd vowed to never take Banks for granted and had tried to do all the things she could to make his life easier, too. She'd decorated their home. She'd made sure the main meals were ready for him at any hour after his meetings. She'd even taken up golf because Banks loved golf.

It was all part of their easy, sweet companionship—the foundation she had come to rely on.

But in the days after she revealed her darkest secret, Banks receded from her life.

They lived in the same home, and yet they barely acknowledged one another. She brightly greeted him when he came home from the club, but he started coming home later and later.

Where he had once let her know his schedule so she could plan around it, these days Banks came and went without touching base. He moved out of their bedroom and into the guest suite. She hoped that was temporary, but as the days wore on, she realized it was not.

She tried to start a conversation and get him to talk about how he felt.

Banks' answers were short, polite, but definitive.

"I do not want to talk about this with you."

"I'm late for a meeting."

"My tee time's in fifteen minutes."

He was never cross. She actually wished he were. Maybe a good knock-down, drag-out fight would help them move forward. But that wasn't Banks.

She tried to go on as normal—to no avail. Their home, once warm and safe and loving, was cold.

After she returned from Blair's appointment, she wrote a letter. She packed a bag. And she made a phone call.

She was traveling surprisingly light for what she was about to do.

But Joetta Armstrong didn't need everything in her closet— she was the queen of a capsule wardrobe when need be. Picking chic outfits with an old money aesthetic; well, she was good at that, and it only required one suitcase. She was, in fact, old money. Jessie called her style quiet luxury. She had evolved to that. Oh, the mini dresses she used to have! Alas. No heart reply from Banks meant it was time to go.

And she had a place to go to: the Kelly girls took her call. And those girls were tough, resilient, and ready to take her in, warts and all. She owed Bruce for that. They were amazing adults. Her luck held on that front.

It was time to do something drastic; hopefully, it would save her marriage.

Banks didn't use email. Banks didn't really do anything but text with her in terms of technology. The letter would be placed on his side of the bathroom sink in the guest suite.

He would see it when he came home. He always washed up in the bathroom before coming down to dinner.

Darling Banks,

I think you need time to process what I told you. I need time too. It was foolish of me to think we could easily, quickly, and happily go back to normal. I'm going to leave for a little while so that you have time to think. I pray you can forgive me, but I also am not selfish enough to try to keep you tied to me. Because the me you know isn't the real me. Or rather, it isn't the total me. The complete Joetta Armstrong is much more of a mess than I ever let you know.

I'm going to tell our daughters that you and I are taking a break —and that it's all my fault, because I know it is. I know that you are the love of my life. I hope that I am the same for you.

If it's time for you to move on without me, I understand. It breaks my heart, but I understand. If you get to a point that you want to talk to me about this—or yell at me about this—whatever you want, you know where to find me.

Love always,
Joetta

· · ·

She drew a heart after her name.

It wasn't that he hadn't responded to her single text yesterday, it was just the sign she'd needed, is all.

Blair was healthy; that was the main thing to focus on. Her daughter was about to make her a six-time grandmother! She had a long way to go to connect with Sawyer, Katie, and Tyler, but hopefully, she'd get there. OOH, the presents she was going to buy for all of them. That was another thing that put a smile on her face, making up for all the lost time.

And seeing the second chance to get it right with Blair's little nugget, as the girls called it.

Joetta got in her car and drove from her gated country club community to Haven Beach.

Ali, of all people, welcomed her with open arms as she pulled in.

"Mom."

That was new. Calling her *Mom*.

As much as her life was in total disarray, the idea that her three Kelly girls called her *Mom* felt like more than she could ever ask for.

But she had one more big thing to do.

She had to tell the twins. Jessie and Jamie, her second-chance family.

Ali settled Joetta into a room at The Sea Turtle Inn. They were doing a ton of work on the place, but the inspector had cleared the north wing for habitation. Habitate she would.

Ali left her to freshen up and made her promise to join her at the Grand Finale. Ali was innately in tune with others, and her oldest daughter didn't press her about Banks. Joetta told her she would love to attend the Grand Finale. This gave her some time.

She had to get the truth ball rolling again.

She had a group chat with her girls. That was as good a place as any to start.

Jamie was overseas and didn't respond. That was typical.

Jessie was going a million miles an hour. That was also typical. But eventually, Jessie called her back.

"What's going on? This text—what's it about?"

"Well...your father and I are separating for a while."

"What are you talking about?"

Jessie loved the perfect image of her nuclear family. Everything about Jessie was about image and perfection. This was about as imperfect as a person could be. It was time her daughter realized her mother was far from perfect.

"Honey, the reason your dad and I are separating right now is that he's having a really hard time with a lie that I told."

"A lie you told. Stop being so dramatic."

"Listen. I have a big thing to tell you, and I think we should do it in person."

"I don't have time right now. Today's crazy."

"Right. How about you come meet me at Haven Beach tonight?"

"I can't tonight—I've got...so tomorrow?"

"Tomorrow works."

"I've got to take Hairy Garry to the vet, and then I've got a two o'clock Zoom, but yeah—lunch will work. All the way down at Haven Beach?"

"Yes, Haven Beach. And just so you know—I can't really prepare you for the shock you're going to have."

"Mom, you're scaring me."

"It's not scary, but it's definitely going to...well, 'shock' is the best word."

"Are you okay?"

"I'm fine."

"You're not sick, are you?"

"No. But it's a jaw-dropper, for sure."

"Fine. I'll see you at lunch tomorrow at Haven Beach."

"All right. I'll text you the restaurant."

"Sounds good."

So, there it was. She was about to tell her children—hopefully easier than telling Banks—but who knew how they'd react? It was the most outlandish story, even though it was true.

Ali popped in with some fresh towels.

"Do you need anything else? We're still quite the construction zone; I apologize for that."

They had fragile but growing warmth between them.

"It's the Presidential Suite! I'm honored."

She was. This was a huge favor from the daughter she'd hurt the most. Ali had taken all of it; she'd been the de facto mother to Faye and Blair. She'd also been the one fueling this dream at The Sea Turtle. Ali was a marvel. Joetta was so proud of her, even though she could claim zero of the credit.

"How's the foundation coming?" Joetta's capital investment had saved the resort, but it was nothing. It was a drop in the bucket when it came to how much she felt she still wanted to give the Kelly Sisters.

"Well, that work is done, but I think they're doing some roofing in a day or two. If it gets too loud, I'll have Sawyer put a chair on the beach any time you need a little break."

"Thank you, honey, I'm fine. See you at sunset."

"Okay, see you at sunset."

Joetta's heart was full of love and also heavy with fear. Her once predictable daily existence now held a surprise around every corner.

Which was the good news and the bad news all at once.

Three

JESSIE

She had a limited window. Making time for her mother for lunch wasn't on her list, but her mother knew how to pull the guilt lever.

"I've only seen you on your Instagram stories over the last month!"

This couldn't be true. How was that true? When her children were babies, she called her mother multiple times a day.

"How do you get them to burp when they seem like they want to but don't?"

"Lay her on your lap."

"What is that little white mark in her mouth?"

"Oh, honey, I think that's thrush; you need to call the doctor."

"Mom, I'm so tired, can you come over?"

And her mother would be there within twenty minutes. She'd play with the girls. She'd put dishes in the dishwasher. She'd do anything to give Jessie a little break.

But now the girls were in school, no longer babies. They were in dance class, Girls on the Run, and Scouts.

Jessie was a glorified chauffeur between her content creation. Somehow, she didn't call her mom as much.

Had it been a month since she'd seen her? Jessie looked at her phone, and sure enough, Mom and Dad were at the recital a month ago. That was the last time she'd seen her mother in person.

Jessie didn't really want to drive all the way out to Haven Beach, but maybe she could take a few ocean videos. Could she use those for content somehow? Maybe a sunscreen brand deal? Or beach cabana or, well, she'd think of something.

She had about two hours between getting all the way out here and back in time to pick the girls up from school and take them to dance. She didn't really want to eat crab cakes on the beach. If you lived in Florida, you never went to the beach, she realized. Who had time for the beach?

The Shack was cute, she had to admit, super cute. A perfect place for lunch if you were on vacation, she surmised. Or retired like her mother. Though retired was generous to say. She only ever worked as a homemaker and for Daddy at the club. It wasn't really a job, was it?

Her mother didn't understand Jessie's schedule. Mom always had a housekeeper, a groundskeeper, and Daddy. Jessie didn't, which was fine, but her mother didn't understand how much it all took to keep up this appearance.

Ugh, okay. Enough. She'd have lunch with her mother and then get back on track with her life.

The Seashell Shack was packed, and people were enjoying the surf and the sand. A little tension in her shoulders relaxed. Oh, to have a life where she could just vacation without making content. She kept the girls out of the videos but also had to let people know she was a mom; it was a balancing act. Every "getaway" they'd had courtesy of her sponsored deals meant she was working and also trying to make memories for her girls. It was exhausting, but it was for her family, so she was determined to make those trips happen.

A good-looking older man greeted her. He had a dazzling smile. He seemed vaguely familiar, but she couldn't place him.

"Welcome, I'm Henry, beachside seat yourself, if you'd like, indoors, I can grab you a table."

"Hi, uh, I am meeting my mom, uh, the name's Armstrong."

"Oh, sure, yeah, Joetta is outside, let me take you."

This guy knew her mom, like on a first-name basis? That was weird. Mom usually stayed close to her own kind at the club. A casual fish joint on the beach? No. Not Mom's usual vibe, but whatever.

She followed Henry through the restaurant and out to the picnic tables on the beach. The salt air was so different from that at home. That long bridge over the bay, and they may as well be in a different universe. The sun wasn't oppressive here; it was warm, almost glowy.

Maybe she needed to get out to the beach more often? When that would fit in, she had no idea.

There was her mom, looking different, looser, dare she say younger?

She wondered if her mom was on a new diet or skin care plan. The tightly coiffed signature bob of Joetta Armstrong usually framed her jawline. Today, it dusted her shoulders. Maybe that was it; the longer hair was so out of character. The breeze had tousled her normally razor-sharp cut. It was so different, but it suited her.

Her mother stood up and opened her arms; Jessie hugged her mom. She inhaled the Chanel No. 5.

That was the same, familiar, classic Joetta Armstrong. At least some things stayed the same.

"You are too thin, way too thin." Her mother was an almond mom, but to hear her say she was too thin? That was upside down. Nothing made her Boomer mom happier than skinny daughters, but now it was the opposite. This was upside down for sure.

She didn't want to unpack that skinny comment. Lately,

people have been saying that. It was getting on her nerves. Her views depended on her looking a certain way, and that was thin.

She was fine, and she waved her mother's concern off.

"Look who's talking, the original almond mom."

"What's an almond mom?"

"Nothing, don't worry about it. I'm not too thin."

"Hmm, well, I'm just glad to see you in person. If you don't mind, your sister is going to FaceTime with us."

Jamie was in the military; she was currently stationed at Aviano Air Base in Italy. Jamie had entered the Air Force Academy after high school. And while she loved flying, she had, over time, gravitated to her passion, dogs.

Jessie loved her sister more than any human outside her children. They were fraternal twins but couldn't be more different. While Jessie was too skinny, cared about hair, makeup, and fashion, Jamie didn't care a lick about any of that. She was dark-haired and gorgeous without a speck of makeup; she looked like she had a glamor filter on at all times.

Their total opposite looks and demeanor fostered a bond and never a competitive instinct. Jessie was so proud of Jamie.

Jamie Armstrong was currently in charge of the K9 units for most of the European bases. It was impressive, specialized, and it kept her away from them most of the time. This was one of her mother's biggest complaints over the years. And to be honest, Jessie's too; they all missed Jamie's physical presence in their lives.

"Okay, so I just accept this request, and then we will be in business."

Watching her mother work her iPhone was like nails on a chalkboard. Jessie was about to grab her mother's phone and just do it herself, but to her surprise, her mom managed to accept the FaceTime request, put the phone on speaker, and set it up with her little pop socket case.

This was also new. When did her mother get a Pop-Socket?

"Wow Mom, you have learned how to use the iPhone after a decade of driving us nuts with it."

"Oh, hush, if I didn't know how to work this thing, I'd never see you or your sister. Hello, Jamie!"

"Hi Mom, hi Jess."

Jess was in a large hangar, it appeared. She was always working; maybe it ran in the family for both of them.

"Girls, I'm so glad you could both do this. I have a pretty big—well, two pretty big things to tell you."

Jessie was used to her mother being dramatic. She expected her mom to say she just decided to switch from Transitional to Coastal décor, or that she and Daddy weren't going to Europe this summer, but rather Mexico.

Mother wanted to make a grand announcement, but a text would do. But Jessie had to stop thinking this way; it was a gorgeous lunch on the beach. She could deal with a little manufactured drama. Heck, she owed Joetta this, since she had been neglecting her lately.

"Two announcements! I'm underdressed," Jessie teased.

"Sorry Mom, I only have a fifteen-minute window here. Can we get the Cliffs Notes on the announcements?" Jamie said.

It was sort of hard to hear her with the surf noises all around them, but Mom had insisted on the time and place for this announcement lunch. Jessie tried not to lose patience. She needed to do a million other things: the girls' new character shoes, the package pick up for the skin care brand she just made a deal with, and the oil change light was on in her vehicle. This side quest wasn't fitting into her go-go-go day.

"Okay, well, I need to warn you that this is going to shock you, and I hope you both can forgive me. It's about my past."

"What, you belonged to another country club before Dad?" Jessie said, and she heard Jamie laugh. Their mother didn't have a past. She had a life of privilege that she'd worked hard to maintain, sure, but a past? She must be watching too many reruns of Knots Landing.

"No, please, girls, this is serious." Her mother paused for dramatic effect. Then Joetta continued.

Oh brother, she's laying it on thick.

"Before I married Daddy, well, I was married before."

Jessie shook her head to try to hear better.

"You're kidding, you had a husband before Dad?" Jessie asked.

"I did, and I had, I have, three other children."

At this point, Jessie had a huge alarm bell in her head.

Did she just say three other children?

Was her mother battling some cognitive decline? Was making up weird stories a sign of aging? Her mother looked great, but what if something was malfunctioning in her brain? Other children?

Joetta's eyes were clear as she continued to unspool a fanciful tale that was so far from what Jessie thought her mother had summoned them for, as to be completely bonkers.

"I have three daughters. We lived in Toledo, Ohio. Then…well, my first husband kept them from me, for his reasons. I was a bad mom, and well, he has passed on, and finally, after all these years, I've reunited with my older girls." Joetta had gone from hesitation and drama to almost a manic state. She was piling on unbelievable sentence after preposterous detail.

"Mom, this is the most bananas thing I've ever heard. I'm at work here…Jessie, is she uh, okay?" Jamie clearly had the same thoughts going through her head as Jessie did. Their mother had dropped her basket, and the yarn balls of her mind were bouncing across the floor.

"She looks fine, needs a haircut," Jessie addressed her sister on FaceTime and then turned back to their mother. "Mom, this is delusional. I'm calling Dad, you shouldn't drive."

"I'm living here, that's the other announcement. Your Dad and I have separated."

At this point, Jessie lost her own composure.

"Mom, this is nuts! You have three mystery daughters? And you're telling us that you and Dad are separated?"

"Yes, that's what I'm telling you." Joetta returned to some semblance of calm after her rambling delusion of a moment ago.

"Is someone trying to scam you on Facebook?" Jamie offered.

That made some sense; maybe their mother had fallen prey to some internet scam. These "daughters" were trying to get money?

"No, this isn't a scam, and I left your father because he is taking this really badly, and he needs time. I hope, in time, we can work it out. But I need space. I need to connect with my past, my daughters, and I hope you two can also. Ali, Faye, and Blair are so amazing and—"

They *have* names, these faux scammy daughters?

Jessie interrupted her mother's crazy rambling. "Mom, this is too much. I think we need to go to the E.R., you're having a stroke." This was the only explanation, other than rapid-onset dementia.

"Call Daddy, ask him," Joetta told her. "Or come with me over to The Sea Turtle Resort. That's where I'm staying. My oldest, Ali, runs the place."

Jessie pinched her nose to try to stem the pounding headache that had developed since her mother's "announcements" began.

"Mom, give the phone to Jessie," Jamie said. Their mother complied.

"Take me off speaker." Jessie did and put the phone to her ear.

"I literally have to get to a meeting," Jamie said. "Get the names of these people, and I'll run some checks."

"You're thinking what I am?"

"Scam, yes for sure. Okay, put me back on speaker."

Joetta Armstrong sat quietly while Jessie and Jamie looked at her like she was speaking in tongues.

"Mom, I love you. I have to go. Do not give any money to these daughters, that's all I can say."

"Too late, I'm in business with them, at the resort I mentioned."

"What?" Jessie was losing her temper now; their mother was off the rails!

"This isn't something I need your permission for. I have a lot to make up for with all of my family. I hope you all can forgive me, but you two have had everything. My other three? Well, they didn't, and I'm going to be sure that I'm there however they need me."

Their mother stood up and addressed Jamie on the phone.

"Honey, run as many checks as you want, and both of you, call your dad. I'll be here, on the beach, ready to talk, or whatever you need. But this is real, and I'm sorry. There was just no other way to tell you but like this, all at once."

"Mom, I can't with this," Jessie said. "I have to get back to get the girls from dance."

"It's okay, I'm only a few feet away. I'll text you both the address. When you're ready, come over, and we can have snacks on the beach. Your girls would love it!"

With that, Joetta Armstrong and her announcements kissed Jessie on the cheek and left her sitting at the picnic table, mouth open, and mind racing.

"I'll call you after I do some legwork," Jamie said.

"Yeah, okay." Jessie had almost forgotten her sister on the phone. She watched her mother kick off her shoes and walk into the sand. She gave a wave of the hand, and Jessie, paralyzed by the news and the moment, sat there, with no idea what to do next.

Henry, the nice man who'd shown her the table, came up.

"See you at the Grande Finale," he yelled out to Joetta.

Joetta yelled back, "Yep, making a really delish pesto for tonight."

"Sounds great," Henry called back to her mother. Her totally nutty mother.

Jessie witnessed the exchange. The Grand Finale? All of a

sudden, her mother, whom she knew better than she knew anyone, seemed like a complete stranger.

"You know my mom?" Jessie asked the nice man.

"Yes, she's an amazing person," Henry said, and if it wasn't in the middle of the day, Jessie would have ordered a double margarita.

As it was, she already felt like she was Alice and she'd tumbled through the looking glass.

Four

BLAIR

Blair had not envisioned the appointment going this way. In her young-twenties fantasies, she and her loving husband would joyfully go to the ultrasound and discover the news: it was a boy, or it was a girl, or something equally magical. It was a scene she'd watched a million times on a million different movie screens. It never looked like this.

Blair was playing the hand she was dealt. Wasn't that what everyone had to do? She had to find the magic her way, with her own life, not Hallmark's version that had been burned into her head.

That meant she was going to be a single mother. And she was going to make as magical a movie as any movie, her own movie.

It also did not mean she was alone. She had several candidates to go with her to this appointment—two sisters, a long-lost mother, and even her new best friend, Ford. In the end, she decided to ask Faye. Her middle sister was the least sentimental, and for some reason, that was exactly what Blair wanted in this moment. Lately, it felt like her emotions were always right at the surface, always ready to bubble over—and they weren't bad emotions. They were just a lot.

Every time she saw a mother pushing a stroller, she had to fight a silly grin. Every time she saw a Pottery Barn catalog with nursery items, she reacted as if she'd never seen a crib in her life. And every time she saw mashed potatoes from Kentucky Fried Chicken, she practically broke out in a dance.

She wasn't even a Kentucky Fried Chicken fan...except, apparently, the little nugget was. So, she kept DoorDash on speed dial and knew exactly the distance to the local KFC. If that's what the nugget wanted, that was what the nugget would get!

Her sister Faye always knew how to lighten a situation, and she was also the person in Blair's immediate family who had been pregnant most recently—Sawyer being the youngest of the nephews and nieces. Faye jumped at the chance.

Faye showed up at the cottage—these days driving the Grotto's pickup truck—a good bit earlier than Blair had told her to arrive.

"I had a couple of deliveries to make, and I thought I'd get that done before I picked you up. It got done early. Can I help you do anything around here?"

Her sisters were babying her; it was in their nature to do that. She didn't mind lately, when napping was becoming something she relished, and housework was not.

But she didn't have a thing to clean or pick up in the beach cottage at the moment. She was focused on the appointment.

"Okay, how's your bladder doing?" Faye asked.

Blair had required the recommended amount of liquids, and at this point, the discomfort was bearable but just barely.

"I'm fine. I just don't want to talk about it. Try not to hit any potholes."

"Well, that's one good thing about living here. Much fewer potholes."

"True."

They loaded into the truck and made their way to the office.

Luckily, the staff understood that a pregnant woman who needed to use the facilities should not be left waiting. Before long, Blair was back in the room with cold jelly on her rapidly expanding bump. Faye held her hand as they watched the amorphous blobs on the screen.

"Do you know what you're seeing?" Blair asked.

Faye said, "I can tell you right now it is a very good-looking genius-level intelligence, uh, blob."

The ultrasound tech laughed at Faye's description as she moved the wand over her belly, and the blob morphed from one gray-looking rounded cloud-shaped thingy into another.

"Are you doing any big gender reveals? Do I need to put it in an envelope and have someone else open it? We're very used to keeping it a secret and then letting you have your big reveal moment." The tech explained the procedure.

Faye and Blair looked at each other. Did she want a gender reveal party or an exploding cupcake? She decided quite quickly; she knew exactly the answer.

"Actually, no," Blair said, looking at the tech.

"There have been a lot of surprises in my life this last year. I'd like to be somewhat prepared for this one if I could."

"Sure, gotcha. These gender reveals get more and more elaborate every day. I've got to ask, as you know. I had a couple who hired a marksman to shoot a clay pigeon filled with blue powder for their reveal, and then an actual bird got in the way, and well, let's just say it was a real mess."

Faye shot Blair a wide-eyed look. The horror! No, no gender reveal here. Blair decided she wasn't into the spectacle, and the surprise of the pregnancy was surprise enough.

The tech continued, "Nice heartbeat. Looking great. Your doctor will give you the full report, of course."

The tech slid the wand over her belly.

"Wait a second, here we go. You want to know, – because I can tell you?"

"Yes, please."

Faye reached her hand out, and the two sisters took a breath in unison.

"I can say definitively: it's a girl." The tech pointed to an area on the screen, but in all honesty, Blair still didn't know what she was looking at until she did. A rounded little baby girl's head!

"A girl? Are you sure?" Blair asked, and Faye squealed, squeezing her hand.

"A girl! Another Kelly Sister—or Kelly Cousin, right?" Faye said, and Blair saw tears glisten in her sister's eyes.

"It's been a while since we've had a girl baby in the family," Blair said. She tried to process all the things being a girl mom would mean.

"It's true. It has been," said Faye.

Blair thought about what it would be like to be the mother of a baby girl. She imagined all the girly things...then realized it could be all the sports things too. Who knew? She looked at Faye; Faye was now openly crying.

"Wait a second. I brought you because you're the least sappy one, I know!"

"I know, right? It's amazing. What a miracle."

And Blair agreed. It really was a miracle. She was forty years old. She had thought this part of her life was never going to happen, that it would remain an unrealized dream. She had never found the right man—which, in hindsight, might've been a blessing—and she had never been able to get pregnant.

Well...she still hadn't found the right man, but according to the tech, everything was looking good for her baby girl. Her daughter, the nugget, is growing just as she should, despite all the obstacles in the way of this happening. It was happening.

On the drive home, Blair—mercifully not in desperate need to pee at that moment—turned to her other obsession: Kentucky

Fried Chicken mashed potatoes. Faye drove the truck straight through the drive thru. Before they could even get back to The Sea Turtle, Blair was digging in. She was starving.

"So, no more nausea, huh?" Faye asked.

"No, not a bit. I'm just generally randomly hungry for these mashed potatoes."

"Okay, well, good thing we've got the KFC."

"Yeah, good thing. I was also chewing ice cubes the other day."

"Oh, that's weird...but not as weird as when I was pregnant with Sawyer. I wanted to put gas in the car and smell the gas. I think they're called pica cravings."

Blair nodded. "Yeah. The human body. It's almost like it's not mine. It's like the nugget is telling my body what it needs."

"Well, as it should be. A little girl! Do you think you'd want to tell everyone tonight at the grand finale?"

"Maybe so, Auntie, maybe so."

"I just want to thank you. I'm so honored you asked me to come with you." Faye paused. "So...not to rain on your parade..."

"But you're gonna ask me about Blake, right?"

"Yeah."

"I mean, he's in the dark so far, and I have the PPO. I have mostly been avoiding the subject."

"You've got a lot to figure out."

Blair sighed. "Right now, though, all I can think about is keeping this little nugget safe and happy."

"You know we're here for whatever. Don't worry about Blake if you don't want to. I did it, you can too."

That was another reason she had asked Faye—she understood what it was like to be a single mom. And what it was like to not have even the option of the father being a part of things. Blake didn't get to be a part of this miracle.

"Whatever you want to do, you've got the whole family on your side. This sweetie will have everything a princess deserves." Blair knew that, still, there was an ache, a worry in her chest, that wouldn't go away. That came to her at night when her mind had a moment to wander. Could she make Faye's prediction true?

Was she enough?

"Thanks. Let's change the subject. How's our big sister doing?"

"Well, amazing actually. I walked in on her and Henry sharing a soda over at the Morning Bell. It's like they're teenagers."

Blair laughed. "Well, I'm glad to see my big sisters have productive love lives."

"Well, the love of *your* life is going to be completely different in a few months."

"True. And I wouldn't have it any other way."

"Okay, so we need to talk to Katie about turning one of the cottages into a nursery/cottage."

"I don't know...I don't know where my long-term living situation is going to be."

"Look—we've got a full hotel that we own, and six cottages."

"I can't stay in the cottages forever."

"True. But for now, they're not fully booked."

That was another thing Blair had to get going on—helping Ali get the cottages fully booked while the inn was under construction was a key mission for her part of running this business.

"Oh, and guess what?" Blair decided to try again, to move the focus off her current confusing future.

"What?"

"Mom has moved into the inn."

"You're kidding me! Why didn't I notice?"

"Oh, it just happened."

"What about her husband?"

"Yeah...Mom left Banks. So maybe it'll be a hotel for wayward single women."

"Maybe," Faye said. "Did she explain why she left him?"

"I haven't had a real long talk with her. Ali was telling me about it because Ali, of all people, offered Mom the inn. So that's where she is."

"Wow. Okay. So, Ali is forgiving Mom *and* dating. It's like we live in the upside-down world."

"I know, right? It's pretty cool."

"It sure is. All right, you've had the mashed potatoes. Anything else before I take you home?"

"Actually...I have to stop at the potty again."

"You're kidding me."

"Nope. This rest stop up here is pretty nice." Blair now knew where to go for her frequent potty requirements these days.

"All right, as you wish."

Faye drove to the rest stop of Blair's choosing.

Faye may be opinionated and headstrong, but she knew not to get between a pregnant woman and her potty breaks!

Five

JOETTA

Joetta looked out the window of the Frank Sinatra residential suite. It sounded a lot fancier than it was, and it was a lot less fancy than she was used to.

There was a small balcony with a chair and a table. She decided to walk out and sit down.

She couldn't remember—prior to her girls coming back into her life—a time when she took time to enjoy this beach. They enjoyed the club. They loved their pool. But living only a few miles away from the beach made it front of mind, or something they could always do when they had time. Somehow, they never had time. And this beach, well, it had mixed memories. It was good, but also the scene of a pivotal decision she didn't even know she was making. Decades away from those moments when she looked at Bruce through the eyes of an innocent girl. She had blocked out the memories, but now, here, she let them in, at least a little.

Bruce was handsome, rugged, and grown up. She was enthralled that he wasn't fawning over her; she chased him. That had never been the case with any boy. And that was the difference: he was no boy. But she, at heart, was a stupid girl. And she'd made giddy moves in a sun-soaked summer. The early '70s were a different planet in her mind, much less a different beach.

Joetta was working hard to earn forgiveness from her daughters. But she knew there were more mistakes that no one would, or should, ever forgive.

Joetta had looked at her phone no less than five times since she'd woken up that morning. Granted, Banks wasn't very good with his cell phone, but still—he had not reached out to her. He had not called her. She didn't know if her marriage was over or if it was just on pause.

In 1974, at sixteen, she'd walked along this beach without a care in the world. That had to be the last time she didn't have a care in the world. She had a lot of cares right now, but living with someone who didn't want her? She'd been down that road once before. That was one thing she didn't have to do again. Despite how much she loved Banks, it wasn't enough for two.

She had lied to Banks about the Kelly Sisters.

She had lied within an inch of her life, and that lie was now exposed. Her Armstrong Daughters were not thrilled. In fact, they were reeling. The twins were conspiring to understand it, explain it, and debunk it. Joetta knew that. The Twins were a unit, and they'd always banded together to deal with the world.

She supposed it would be like having the rug pulled out from under you to find out your mother was a completely different person than you thought she was. Joetta was the keeper of secrets, the puller of the rug. Since Bruce, she'd been the one in charge.

She wondered—had she been a completely different person for decades? She had lived two realities, two lives. There was the life she'd had with Banks, and there was the life she'd left with Bruce.

Bruce had been the enemy for so long, but looking at Ali, Faye, and Blair, she had softened. It was a fuller story than Bruce was the enemy, and she was the victim.

And what did it really matter now—who caused what? Bruce was gone, and she was here, trying with all her might to make things right.

She hoped she could get the twins to forgive her or at least accept what she had told them. Currently, Jessie and Jamie appeared to believe that she had been scammed—that the Kelly girls just wanted her money.

That was not true. In fact, Ali had practically kicked her out when she showed up the first time.

But now, on the plus column, the Kelly Sisters and Joetta were a family—a wobbly, brand-new, doe-on-spindly-legs type of family —but a family, nonetheless.

She would have to do a lot of work to get all five girls to be part of her life. But as long as no more of her lies came to light, maybe —just maybe—she could do it.

Her lies.

She wished above everything else that she could be one Joetta, live one life.

But she knew there was still a lie that could blow apart whatever progress she had made with The Twins—or with Banks, if Banks came around.

She picked up her phone one more time and looked.

No messages from Banks.

No missed calls.

At this point, he would know she had moved out.

The question was—did he care?

JESSIE

After the revelation her mother had dropped on Jessie and Jamie, Jessie was momentarily paralyzed.

She had watched her mother walk down the beach toward the resort. There was no way—no form, no how—she was heading to The Sea Turtle, or whatever it was called. After her mother waved and disappeared from sight, Jessie picked up her phone again and called Jamie.

"Girl, I said I had a meeting," Jamie said.

"I know, but what the heck?"

"Look, I've got about five more minutes before I have to be in front of Colonel Walker with my monthly report."

Jessie knew Jamie loved her job. Training animals was her calling in life. Jessie had never found her own calling but loved that her sister had found hers.

"Just clocking this with you. So, the Mom's being scammed theory?"

"Yeah?" Jamie said.

"All this money she gave for this hotel, this flea trap...that must be part of it."

"Well, how do we know it's a flea trap?"

"I don't know. I'm just guessing."

"Well, it's her money."

"Well, no. It's Dad's money.

"Actually, you know Mom's family was loaded—just as much as Dad's," Jamie corrected her.

Jessie always thought of Dad as the deep pocket and Mom as the arm candy, but Jamie was right. That wasn't really true. "I guess," she conceded. "Still, this whole story is bananas."

Jessie could not wrap her head around the fact that her mother had a secret life before them—so secret that she lived in, of all places, Toledo, Ohio.

"I just feel bad for Dad in all this," Jessie sighed.

Jamie agreed. "Yeah. I'm sure he is totally wrecked. I'm going to call him later and just check in."

"Good idea," Jessie said.

"Right. So, I'll do a little investigation to make sure Mom isn't being scammed. Like you said, we don't know anything about these...these other daughters," Jamie said. "And I can do that from here."

"Good idea," Jessie said.

"All right. I'll visit Dad later to make sure he's okay, and I'm going to figure out how to keep these alleged sisters from causing any more trouble."

"Okay, sis. Gotta go."

"All right. Bye-bye."

Jessie and Jamie were fraternal twins. They looked nothing alike. Jamie didn't look like anyone in the family.

But everyone said Jessie looked exactly like Joetta. Joetta the liar, or Joetta the deluded, or was it Joetta the victim of a scam? All of these things seemed possible. Did her mother have Alzheimer's? Was this the first sign? Jessie had had a pit in her stomach lately. Her appetite had been almost zero anyway, and now this.

She got in her car and listed in her head all the different things she needed to do for tomorrow's content.

Then she saw the clock.

"Oh no."

She had to get across town to the dance studio to pick up her girls. The last thing she needed was her husband complaining that she was distracted, and the girls whining that she was late. She always felt late. She always felt under the gun. She never felt she was in the spot she was supposed to be.

Would that ever change?

She doubted it.

She pulled down the sleeves of her linen blouse. She had another nasty-looking bruise. Lately, the slightest thing caused huge, ugly black splotches.

Jessie knew she needed to go to the doctor, knew she needed to figure out her marriage, knew she was one wrong move from losing it. But she didn't know how to stop any of it.

Seven

BLAIR

Blair looked at the booking calendar. Once Ali had accepted help from her baby sisters and their mother, she'd also been incredibly open to collaboration on how to get this business in the black.

The three sisters had come up with a plan to divide the herculean task of turning the ramshackle resort into something that would sustain them and guests for decades to come.

Ali was a manager, to her core. She could fix roof tile and wield a power tool if need be, but her core strength was coordinating the resources, getting the best price, understanding construction schedules, and putting systems in place. She also understood how to create experiences for potential guests. Since they were under construction to get the cottages and the inn up to code, which had to happen before they could consider décor and shiny things, Ali was going to be busy with that for a while.

That left a million other tasks to manage, and Blair stepped in with her strengths. She was managing the budget, the finance portion of the projects. Thanks to Mom, they had the capital to fix what needed fixing, but just barely. They still needed to bring in guests, and further, they would need to fill the rooms and cottages the second they were ready for occupancy. And at that point, Joetta's money would run out, and they would need cash flow. This had to be sustainable. One thing this pregnancy had done was galvanize Blair's resolve. She would make this work; she had to support the nugget, and she would.

If Ali were the CEO, Blair would be the Chief Marketing and Finance Officer! Along with eating whatever the nugget required, drinking water, and walking on the beach, every other waking moment was filled with delving into strategies for marketing The Sea Turtle.

She also managed the calendar. If Ali's construction schedule stayed on target, Blair knew precisely which days which room would be ready for occupancy, and her mission was to make sure that they would be.

They had an intricate set of projects and dates, but Blair was doing everything she could to be sure that, once a room was ready, they'd be hosting guests.

Sister Faye was in for all the exterior landscaping, and with Sawyer was managing the pool upgrade. Faye was also working on making sure they had what they needed to lure brides here for a beach wedding or shower venue. They knew this was a prime spot for a gorgeous, if modest-sized, destination wedding.

Faye and her boyfriend Rudy Palmer, or Palmtree, as Blair and Ali teased, was their new favorite Kelly Boyfriend, and the two worked on his list of contacts with the nursery and Faye's burgeoning floral arranging client list to smooth out bare spots in the calendar.

It was all well and good to be booked for Spring Break, but to be filled in September or January, that was the trick, and that was Faye's part of The Sea Turtle's business plan.

The beauty of Blair's role? She could grab her laptop, sit on the deck, and watch the surf roll in while she plotted marketing strategy and managed her spreadsheets. The fact that she might be able to make a life here, in this setting, seemed like the fulfillment of a wish she didn't know she'd made.

She was working on the expenses spreadsheet when Ford Taylor appeared on the steps of her deck.

"How are the plans for world domination?"

"Hello! Well, not the world, just these couple of acres. We will rule the world from here."

"Yes, of course. Up for a little walk?"

Blair and Ali were going to eat dinner at The Shack later and touch base on the million things they had to coordinate, but right now, the idea of flipping closed the laptop and taking a little walk sounded perfect.

"I mean, if you live here and don't get your toes in the sand every day, are you really living?"

"Exactly."

Blair held up a finger to pause Ford and then popped inside the cottage. She placed her computer on the table in the kitchenette and also grabbed her water bottle. Everyone in her life was hyper-focused on her hydration; if she was walking, she was sipping. If nothing else to stop the millions of mother hens, including Ford, who pecked at her in regard to staying healthy.

You pass out one time, and you never hear the end of it!

She closed the cottage door, and there was Ford, patiently waiting for her. He offered her a hand as she took the three wooden steps from the deck to the beach.

"I'm not that unsteady, yet."

"But your little tennis ball is looking more like a basketball; you may be penguin walking before the end of the month."

She smiled and looked down. For the first few months, she had worn her normal clothes; if you looked at her, you wouldn't know she was pregnant. But now, and it almost seemed overnight, Ford was right, the bump was a thing!

"I don't know about basketball, maybe more like a loaf of bread." She patted her tummy, and they made their way out to the water's edge and began walking along the beach. It was a stroll, no longer the run she was trying for when she first moved in.

"I'm telling you, I can't wait to see it when it gets to be beach ball size."

Blair laughed. Beach ball! That would be nuts!

Hanging out with Ford was easy, calming, and peaceful. And he had come to her rescue more than once since they'd met. He was a good friend.

Her sisters ribbed her; they teased that the mogul lifestyle CEO and designer had designs on their little sister. But it wasn't like that. Ford Taylor was her friend, nothing more. He was growing into her best friend, it seemed, but that was the extent of it.

No matter how much her sisters winked and teased her about Blair seemingly accidentally attracting one of the most eligible bachelors on the planet, she knew the truth. No one was interested in her in "that way." She was about to be a single mom with a bananas ex-boyfriend. Not exactly eligible bachelorette territory. Nope, they were in the friend zone, and that was exactly fine with her. It was what she needed.

"Any sign of Blake?" Ford was vigilant in checking in on that since he'd run off an angry Blake a few weeks ago.

"No, he is abiding by the court order. No sign."

"Good, I still wish you'd let me put some security cams around your cottage, but good."

Overprotecting her was everyone's mission, it seemed.

"I'm fine. Let's look at the birds and forget about my questionable life choices."

"Fair. But from where I'm sitting, it seems like you've got life figured out pretty good."

She smiled and agreed. Running a business with her sisters, living on the most gorgeous stretch of beach in the land, making new friends, finding her mother, and waiting for her miracle, it was more than she could have dreamed of even a few months ago.

But although she kept shrugging off questions about Blake, acting as though she wasn't concerned, she was lying. She was very worried about him reappearing. And what he'd do once he found out she was having his child.

Eight

JESSIE

"My husband loves my lasagna! It's one of the favorite things I make for him. As you know, I like to make all my pasta from scratch. So, let's get started."

This was not a livestream, no chance in heck of that.

Jessie inserted file footage she had on her phone of the one time she made the lasagna noodles from scratch. It had taken her forever to do, and there was flour everywhere; they didn't hold together right, and it was, worst of all, not great tasting.

But she had video of her using her pasta maker. That pasta maker was a trade, and it taught her a lesson. You couldn't pay for a dance class with a pasta maker. She learned after that. She needed to be paid a fee for her posts, not a year's worth of body wash or a pasta maker.

Jessie had shots she hadn't used of that pasta disaster that would look okay if she edited it right, so she cut that in first. She used a cheerful voice to describe the process. She credited Ina Garten with her actual tips and then moved on to her sauce.

Jessie wasn't a food content creator and had no desire to secure a cookbook deal.

But she had started the food prep videos because views were down on her hair, makeup, and fashion videos. She literally threw spaghetti at the wall, and views spiked. So, cooking it was. The women meticulously cooking elaborate meals for their families were doing well for other creators. She added cooking to her list of content ideas.

The entire lasagna project took twice as long to shoot and edit for her YouTube channel as it actually did to make. If she'd made it. Which, technically, she didn't.

After she'd shot all the ingredients, she took one more step, a step she did not film. Jessie removed a Stoffer's family-sized frozen lasagna from its foil container, peeled off the plastic, plopped it in a glass pan, dripped some Ragu on the sides so it looked real, and put it in the oven.

When she was done, it would look like she'd cheerfully, easily, layered pasta, sauce, meat, and cheese over and over again to create her husband's favorite meal.

In between each layer, she double-checked her hair, she wiped the counter, she hid any evidence of mess, and she watched the clock. It was her day to get the kids from school and get them to dance.

She peeked in the oven; she used her phone camera and shot a little more video of the lasagna baking. As the cheese bubbled, so did her bitterness. She wasn't making this for her Lando; he hadn't eaten here in two months.

He'd told her that since she seemed to be the only one who could do anything right in the house, she could do it on her own. And she'd definitely agreed. That was a mistake. She didn't think she could. She sure as heck wouldn't tell Landon that. If he wanted to be gone, he could be gone. She wasn't going to chase after him.

This dinner wouldn't go to waste; it would be dinner. Just not a from-scratch dinner. Dinner was a long way off, though. Dinner was after dance, and after they'd done homework, and after she helped them lay out clothes for tomorrow. The fight about what to wear was much better waged the night before than in the morning when the clock was the enemy.

That was something, at least: she'd have dinner all set for them. Lately, she hadn't even been able to accomplish the smallest tasks. She felt like all the plates she normally spun were crashing one by one.

In the hour that the lasagna was cooking, she'd shoot three videos about her haul from Walmart, Amazon, and Target.

Then, if she had time, she'd take them all back before she got the girls.

Jessie couldn't afford to keep these hauls. Not by a mile.

Her primary closet was set up more as a studio than a closet anyway. She had a ring light on a tripod pointing to the space she'd cleared. The walls of the room you could see in the videos were meticulous and curated. She'd taken to shoving the actual mess of her life into Landon's mostly empty closet.

The gap between what she was presenting on her social media and her actual life was getting wider and wider.

Jessie checked her hair, messy bun arranged, "no makeup" in place; she was ready. She hit record, three, two, one.

"Hi! Jessie here, I've got three new looks from Walmart that I think you'll love. They're all centered around looking decent at school pick up, but also with tweaks, good enough to get drinks with Mr. Jessie." On her social media, she protected her family; the girls' faces were never shown, and her husband wasn't Landon; he was Mr. Jessie.

He wanted to be anonymous, and she was living her life online. It was bound to crash, and it sort of had. But she barreled on, with the latest barrel jeans.

"First up, these barrel jeans, I'm loving this cut lately." She noticed the jeans were a little looser on her than the other day. Her mother had been nagging her about her weight when she watched her posts. But Jessie didn't have time to add that to the list of worries. She preached about self-care product hauls; she didn't actually take care of herself.

Jessie put that out of her mind.

She continued talking about the outfit, in detail, and how she'd style it. She put on different shoes, different accessories, and a sweater, and off. She modeled clothes from all the retailers that offered her affiliate commissions.

And she ended the last one by letting her followers know she had a lasagna in the oven. "You know I always keep it real!" A lie.

Jessie carefully put the clothes back in their respective bags, receipts at the ready, tags untucked from when she'd hidden them for the video.

Jessie thought back to before the pandemic. Was that the last time things were okay with her and Landon?

It certainly wasn't okay when they were forced to be in the house all the time together. But they'd lasted through the lockdown and several years after. She'd thought they'd weathered the worst. But as her business as an influencer grew, her marriage shrank.

She almost thought it would be easier if he were in love with someone else. But that wasn't the case, as far as she knew.

"I'm tired of this made-up life, I'm tired of your drive to have everything perfect. Life isn't perfect." Landon had laid out his reason for wanting space from her as he'd packed his bags that day, while the girls were in school.

She didn't argue with him. She didn't fight. She just hoped it would work itself out.

That was the stated reason why he'd packed his bag and moved out. It had the ring of a lie when it happened, though. It had not gone unnoticed by Jessie how many inside jokes he had with his "work wife" when they'd been at the office holiday party last year. It would be easier to blame the "work wife" than blame herself. Maybe they'd fallen out of love, grown in two different directions.

Deep down, though, she worried that she was the cause. That she wasn't enough.

Jessie still believed there was hope. She loved her husband; he was just going through a phase. They could work this out. There was no need to "keep it real" on her TikTok when she knew it could all blow over. So, Jessie had kept up the façade on her videos. She was a loving wife and mother to two beautiful daughters. Her house was chic, her clothes quiet luxury, and her meals were created from scratch.

The only one, other than the girls, who knew she and Landon were living apart was her mother. Her mother had to know since she helped with the girls. Her mother was the one person who had a clue about any of it. She'd always been skeptical about the social media job or air quotes "job." And now it turned out her mother was right.

She'd made her mother promise to keep it a secret. The girls, too, were supposed to be quiet. It was private.

Private. She'd opened up her life to the world, and now that her world was crashing, she didn't know how to say it, how to tell anyone that she had absolutely nothing under control.

It was all falling apart, she was lying with every haul, get ready with me, and day in the life.

She was lying to herself most of all. But she didn't know how to stop it. She wished she'd never created this fairy tale. It was too hard to make believe.

Nine

FAYE

Faye spent the morning working with a new client. It was still weird to say she had clients! But the word of her floral stylings had spread since she'd stepped in to help Rudy out. Blair had her up with Instagram, and she'd been posting her flights of fancy with a link to a tiny one-page contact form. Blair said this was all the advertising she needed right now.

Sawyer was also key in helping her take photos. She'd just finished putting together a wild-looking floral recipe using hibiscus, passionflower, moss, and every deep purple thing she could get her hands on at the nursery. Skyblue Lupine and Blazing Star shot up like spiky rockets from an explosion of deep Spider Lily and Firebush. Faye used moss to drip off the sides of the vase. Sawyer was there to take photos as she tweaked the final Everglades witchy-inspired creation.

"There is no way any bride or event organizer will want this weirdo thing, I'm sure. But I saw the purples that Rudy had here, and well, it spoke to me!"

"Listen to you, my mom, the witchy artistic floral designer, and you said I was living in a fantasy world, trying my hand at ceramics."

Faye didn't have a retort for that; she was still worried about Sawyer's prospects, but she was trying to be better about letting him walk his own path.

"I still say go into welding or be an electrician and then do ceramics as a..."

"As a backup, yes, mother, I know, and no."

Faye suppressed her smothering instinct and returned focus to the project at hand. The bouquet. "I think she's ready."

Faye had been collecting vases from every funky thrift store she could find, and this one looked like it could have come from Norma Desmond's dining room. Perfect for the gothic vibe that had developed from Rudy's leftover stock. She was just as surprised as Sawyer that her practical life and work had morphed into this creative career. She was actually making money with flowers. It was still hard to believe.

Rudy had cleared out a little corner storeroom; she used it as an office and as a studio for Sawyer's photos. He'd set up a backdrop and a dramatic light for his part of this operation. She was grateful for his expertise and that he'd taken this on. Faye wasn't sure if her brain could process any more change. There had been a lot of that in the last year since their father had died. Bruce wouldn't recognize her life; sometimes, she didn't either.

Sawyer got out his camera and got to work.

"Mom, this one might be my favorite."

"You're a sweet kid; you say that every time."

As a single mother, raising a boy, now a man, in today's world, she worried she'd get it all wrong. But the opposite had happened; Sawyer had turned out great. Whether it was her or just his innate positivity—best not to analyze too much—he was a good kid, uh, man. She was an old dog, just trying to keep learning new tricks!

Sawyer took a few photos with his camera and then with his

phone. He had an idea for the high-quality images, something about art prints? She didn't pay too much mind to that, but the phone pictures were what led to clients.

Sawyer took the pics, Blair had researched the hashtags to use, and Faye dutifully posted those each time, along with the captions, which she did herself, along with the actual arrangement, of course.

"Can't wait to see what kind of bride digs this vibe, that would be one fun wedding," Sawyer said and then showed her his phone.

"Wow, if I do say so," Faye replied. Her arrangement looked like something out of a dark fairy tale in the photos. It was what she had in her brain. Somehow, she was able to make it real.

"Good job, Mom. See you at The Turtle?"

"Oh, yes, dang, I need to get moving."

Joetta had asked them all block out a little more time than usual for their bi-weekly business meeting.

They were touching base as sisters and with Joetta ever since they had taken the capital investment. Monday and Thursday in the late afternoon, they'd meet, go over plans, projects, and cash flow, to be sure The Sea Turtle was on track. Faye was the least important to this operation, she determined, but she did have suggestions here and there, and Blair had convinced her that the floral business was going to be an off-season boon for them once they got a good year of data. That was Blair; data was her wheelhouse!

Faye took the fantasy arrangement, put it up in the front near the checkout, with her contact card, another way her client calls were coming in, and she and Sawyer headed to The Sea Turtle.

Sawyer drove, and she posted the Swamp Witch Bouquet, as she decided to call it, to her Instagram feed.

Her phone buzzed immediately.

"Ha! We have a dozen likes in less than one minute. Who knew?"

"I knew, Mom. This one is a showstopper for the magical-minded matrimony."

"Ha, okay, looks like you might be right, now all we need is for some of those likes to fill out the contact form, and we're in business."

"For sure," Sawyer said and gave her a fist bump as they drove along Gulf Boulevard.

It was a short distance to The Sea Turtle. Most days after the meeting, she stayed for the Grand Finale. She also loaded the back of the truck with floral arrangements for the cottages. Ali knew hospitality, and that included mini floral arrangements in each kitchenette and primary bedroom.

Faye had even gotten a booking for a baby shower from one of the guests.

"It's a numbers game," Blair had said. "The more places people see your beautiful work, the more bookings you'll get!"

So far, Ali and Blair had been right. And her flowers were ushering in the sweet smell of success and salt air.

Ten

JOETTA

Didi being away right now was bad timing for Joetta, but good timing for her sister's health. Jorge had agreed that the only way Didi would continue to recover was to stop being so close to The Sea Turtle.

It was impossible for her big sister not to want to help and to work, and to be supportive, and to take absolutely everyone's calls and texts. Joetta called her sister Didi all the time. At least now, when she was on vacation, she screened and then answered. Joetta was part of the problem, but she couldn't help it. Didi was her soulmate, more so than her husband or anyone else on the planet.

This particular call was for moral support and to reassure herself that she was doing the right thing. Even though it felt sometimes like she was burning down all she had built. The fairy tale life she'd concocted was hard to let go of, even though lies were the foundation.

"You will never have the dream family without honesty," Didi said. Her sister was right, annoyingly right.

Still, when she heard the word honesty, Joetta laughed. "I am really tired of honesty."

She was only partly joking. But there was no way to have her Kellys and Armstrongs too, without being honest.

"Look, the worst thing is already out there," Didi said.

"That's true."

Joetta still couldn't believe the joy she felt, the lightness that came into her heart when her three Kelly daughters accepted her back into their lives. It was like losing a boulder-sized weight that had been sitting on her heart. She could finally take a deep breath without a hitch. She had carried around that weight for so long, it had become a part of her, and now that she didn't have it—well, she wasn't quite fancy-free, but she sure did feel lighter.

"You want to keep that feeling going, right?" Didi said.

"I do."

"All right. You are doing the right thing. You need to tell the girls everything." There was a subtext there, Joetta knew.

"Yep," she said, but it was time to change the subject. She shifted the focus to Didi. "How are you doing?"

"Oh, my abs are looking spectacular. Pilates every morning. I'm thinking about doing a 5K."

"Seriously, how are you?"

"Well, I have been taking a yoga class."

Didi and Jorge were on a cruise, and then an island getaway was planned. They would be on holiday for a few more weeks. It was the first time that Joetta could remember her sister ever being on a vacation. Joetta wished Didi were here but knew in the end this was her mess to clean up, not her big sister's.

"I'm glad to hear it. You let Jorge take care of you."

"He's driving me crazy," Didi said.

"Oh, what—being kind, being attentive?"

"Well, yes. I'm not like you. I do not like to be waited on."

"Yeah, I'm definitely starting to realize how much Banks did for me, although I didn't know so much of it—bringing the groceries in or making sure there was enough gas in my car. He was always checking on me." She realized, with Didi gone and Banks checked out, for the first time, she wasn't the center of someone else's universe. She was adjusting. It was probably time she ceded the spotlight anyway.

"Still no word from Banks?"

"No. Radio silence."

"Well, here's the thing. When you get your personal house in order, I'll help you figure out how to get Banks back."

"Sounds too good to be true, that offer. I don't know if we can pull it off. I hurt him pretty good, too."

"Also, the hurt isn't over." Didi was relentless, even on vacation.

"I got it. I'm just at my limit right now, okay. Big changes. Big, honest me. Let me get used to it before I cold-plunge into the next, uh, big secret."

"All right, all right. Time for my water aerobics class. Talk to you soon."

"Don't overdo it."

"Yes, ma'am. That's what I need—more nursemaids," Didi said. "Tell those girls, all five of them, I love them."

"Of course. Oh, and also make sure Ali knows about the return vent in the inn where—"

Joetta cut her off. "Ali will be fine without you micromanaging."

"Yeah, yeah. All right. Water aerobics, it is."

Joetta and Didi hung up the call.

Joetta was meeting her girls around the pool. It would be Joetta, Ali, Faye, and Blair. She loved their bi-weekly meetings. It was so fun to watch them blossom with their individual talents and skills. It was also amazing to see The Sea Turtle come to life bit by bit under their talent and hard work.

She could also see Bruce Kelly in all of them, and somehow it didn't upset her. They knew how to fix things, how to roll up their sleeves, and how to keep a stiff upper lip in the face of adversity. That was Bruce, no question.

She was able to appreciate that the girls were a product of everything that had happened to them, including Bruce Kelly as their father.

Joetta and her Kelly daughters sat at the little table with the umbrella. It wasn't too warm yet in the afternoon. A few months from now, she'd have to pass on outdoor meetings. The girls didn't really realize how hot the Florida summers could get. They'd find out.

She had arranged lemonade glasses for each of them, and they all appeared a few minutes early because, to a woman, they were so conscientious. Maybe that was to Bruce's credit as well. He was a stickler.

She remembered she'd become one too, but back in the day, she'd rebelled against her husband. She pushed back against schedules. She was a baby trying to be an adult and failing back then. Joetta shook her head. It wasn't the time to live in regret. It was time to come clean.

"All right, ladies—"

Before she could continue, Ali started the meeting with a list of things they had to do, along with a list of things they had checked off as completed. Blair weighed in about some advertising she wanted to place, and Faye explained that she had three potential venue clients to meet with in the next few weeks.

Ali's job was the hardest—managing the contractors and making sure that the inn, which needed the most work structurally, was still on schedule. Of course, scheduling—Ali had that locked. She had a light touch but was definitive with everyone who worked with her. She's such a good boss, Joetta thought.

After the business of the day was completed, it was Joetta's turn.

The last thing she wanted to do was derail their work, but she had a dream, and that dream included all of her daughters. So, she started.

"How much do you know about my life since I left Toledo?"

The girls chimed in. They knew she was married to Banks. They knew Banks owned the country club. They knew she had inherited some money from their grandparents. All in all, they knew she was a woman of means, but they didn't know much about her family life.

She was ready to share this part; hopefully, the girls would handle it okay.

"First, I want to say the last few weeks have been the most amazing of my life. I am so grateful to all of you for letting me be a part of this, for accepting me, and for slowly letting me get to know your amazing selves and your amazing children."

It had been incredible for her to find out that she and Sawyer could laugh over drinks. She still hadn't met Ali's children, but the idea that Blair would have a baby—one she would know from the very beginning—well, it was hard for her to even express how much joy she felt about that.

But now she was about to possibly ruin it.

So be it, she thought. *Here goes nothing.*

"I don't know if Didi told you or if you looked me up, but I had two daughters—twins—after I moved back here with Banks."

They piped up. "Yeah, we did kind of know that." They all looked her in the eyes, no sheepishness, and she didn't detect any anger.

God, please let them be okay with this new twist.

"Well, I don't know what you think about that, but I'd really like the three of you to meet the two of them. Well, at least one of them."

"Which one?" Blair said.

"Well, Jessie—Jessica. She is in town, and it would be easy to bring her here. Jamie—

her fraternal twin is in the military, so she's a lot less accessible. Although I'm hearing from Jessie that Jamie is almost done with her current hitch."

Having Jamie home from overseas; that was another dream entirely.

"I just," Joetta continued, "—I would love Jessie to meet the three of you."

The three sisters didn't say much for a moment. It made Joetta very concerned. In fact, they all looked toward Ali. She found that Ali still held a position of de facto mom among them. Of course, in Joetta's own life, her big sister had always been the boss.

Ali was still the boss.

She thought, *Here we go again.*

This was going to be really hard for Ali to open up to. Ali was the most hurt, the most affected by losing Joetta as a mother, by the lies.

Ali leaned forward. She clasped her fingers in front of her. No one said a word. The way Ali went, so went the rest of the Kelly Sisters.

Ali spoke.

"Joetta, I would really love to meet Jessie and Jamie as soon as we possibly can. One thing I've learned in the last—oh—fifty—some years is that there is nothing better than a sister, and what an amazing thing to find. We have two more, even if they are half-sisters."

Joetta didn't expect to cry, but there it was. Tears leaked from her eyes. She tried to swallow them. She tried not to be emotional, but she couldn't help it.

Blair reached out her hand. "Oh, it's all right. Did you think Ali was going to bark or something?"

Ali laughed. "I do have that reputation, apparently."

Faye piped up. "I thought I was the tough one."

"Oh, please, you're a softy," Ali said.

And Joetta glowed under the light of her three daughters and envisioned what it might be like to have all five of them together in this very place.

It was her fondest wish and maybe—just maybe—it could come true.

Even though she knew there was still a lie she would not, could not, reveal.

Eleven

BLAIR

Blair watched their mother walk away toward the inn. Despite the shade and the lemonade, it was getting warm. They had to remember their mother wasn't in her forties or fifties, but rather headed toward seventy. Still, the idea that she even had an internal monologue that said *their mother* put a smile on her face.

"What do you know about that? She came clean without anybody pushing her," Blair said. She was proud of Joetta.

Ali raised an eyebrow. "Yeah, she did. Gotta give her that."

Faye chimed in. "So, we all knew about the two sisters, right?"

"Well, yeah," Blair said. "I had looked her up on different social media and society pages, and they always mentioned the two Armstrong twins. So, I did know—it's not such a shock."

Ali then chimed in. "Yeah, I mean, I think what shocked her— I think the shock for Joetta is that I didn't have a tantrum about it."

"How do you feel about it?" Faye asked.

Blair could see that there was a potential minefield here. The three daughters who got the worst of their mother, and the two daughters who got the best of everything. Could they get along? Did they have anything in common other than the woman who gave birth to them?

But Ali surprised them again.

"The older I get, and after all we've been through, what I can see more than anything else is that it really is about family. It really is about these people that we are connected to. If we can be connected to two more sisters, I don't know. I don't know how it will go. I don't know if we'll get along with them. I mean, let's be honest, these two girls were raised with a silver spoon."

Then Blair chimed in. "Yeah, and we were raised with tinfoil on a TV dinner."

They all laughed.

"But can you imagine? Two more sisters," Blair said. "And thanks to my social media research, I do know that Jessie has two daughters."

Faye chimed in. "Can you believe it? Two more cousins for our kids."

"I know, right? How old are the girls?" Ali said.

"They're young. They are elementary school-aged, from what I could tell," Blair said. Although Jessie was a social media influencer, it looked like she had done a good job of protecting her children from the glare of the Instagram feed.

"Well, maybe they'd like to hang out at the beach sometime," Ali replied.

And the three sisters started to plan.

"We could do pumpkins for Halloween, right? Sawyer is so good at carving pumpkins," Faye said.

Ali chimed in. "And I mean, maybe they'd be good babysitters for the future nugget."

"In the end, we should give Mom some credit," Blair said. "She did tell us. We didn't force her. It had to have been hard."

Ali conceded. "Yeah, I think she really has turned over a new leaf. She wants to make things right. But let's just take it one step at a time. Let's meet Jessie first before we start carving pumpkins."

"Noted," Blair said.

And the girls finished their meeting just in time to get ready for the Grand Finale of the night.

Twelve

JESSIE
2012

The house was a wreck, a straight-up, unadulterated wreck when they bought it. But Jessie loved it. Her mother was appalled, of course.

"Let Daddy and me help you. I mean, Landon is just starting out; this would be sort of a second wedding present."

"No, Mom, we're doing it on our own." She knew her parents had money; she'd always had whatever she needed or wanted as a teen. But as a grown-up, she wanted only Landon and the life they could build together. Not handouts or way too much meddling from Mom.

Landon was his own man; that's what she loved about him. He was just starting at the dealership, and money was tight. This may not be their forever home, but she was determined to make it cute!

The ranch house on Palm Court was built in the 1960s. It was so far away from her style as to be practically on another planet. But with creativity and elbow grease, she knew they could make it something to love. They were a team; he held the ladder, and she rolled the paint!

Landon worked nights and weekends, and she did the same at the spa. But slowly, they were turning the little ranch into something she was proud of. Maybe they'd even flip it!

It was Sunday night, and the dealership was closed, so they had a date with a couple of paint brushes. She'd already taken off all the switch plates, and Landon had brought the ladder in. The "wreck room" was about to get a fresh coat of white paint over the Brady Bunch paneling.

Landon stood at the wall with the roller.

"Okay, you're sure we can paint the paneling?"

"I'm sure, I looked it up, this paint has primer, and this old dark room will look fresh as a daisy after."

"I kind of like this retro, Rockford Files vibe."

She wrinkled her nose. They'd already pulled up a cigarette-stained shag carpet, they'd washed the dirty windows, and now the paint was the last step in rescuing this room.

"I love it when you're totally disgusted," Landon said.

"What?"

"Yeah, that nose thing is the cutest." She laughed. He bopped her nose with the paint roller. It was, of course, filled with paint.

"Landon!" He laughed and put his arms around her. He planted a kiss on her, and now they were both smeared with Sherwin-Williams Alabaster White.

"I thought we were painting," she said as the kiss did not seem to be ending any time soon.

"Nah, let's leave it. This Brady Bunch look is coming back. I feel it. It's about to be the coolest thing, '70s chic."

"Oh, please," she protested. But not for long.

Their home improvement project could wait.

Thirteen

JESSIE

Present Day

The man she'd flipped two houses with, had two babies with, and been in love with for two decades felt like a stranger to her now.

It was still beyond belief that she and Landon were splitting childcare duties, researching alimony and child support, and barely looking at each other without fighting.

To some degree, the separation had shed light on how much Landon didn't know about the details of their actual life. He was seeing that the care, education, and management of June and Joy was a full-time job with a million moving parts.

Where is my hair band?

Where are my dance shoes?

Dad doesn't know which ballroom the rehearsal is in.

Even on weekends that were supposed to be Landon's, she wound up answering a million questions and dropping off missed assignments.

This time, she had to swing by Landon's condo to drop off

June's character shoe and Joy's inhaler. She also had to send Landon a text to the address of the ballroom, and even remind him that June needed to remember her water bottle or else she'd start complaining of a headache. Some kid-free weekend she was having. It would be easier to actually have the kids than to hold Landon's hand through his Daddy Weekend.

A mediator had set up their childcare arrangement. She had complaints. But at the heart of it, Landon was a good dad despite not being the greatest husband lately. He may not know any of the details, but when the girls danced, he was in the audience. When they wanted to play, he got out the games. He had never missed a performance or a teacher conference or a grilled cheese sandwich when one of them had the sniffles. Landon loved them. She used to think he loved all three of his girls. Now she realized it was his two girls. That stung, no doubt. She pushed the feeling aside.

The girls had fun with their dad, not so much with her. It was the classic case of the fun parent and the one who had to actually parent. Maybe if she didn't have to handle all the things, she would be more fun. Landon said she was too controlling, that he felt stifled. It was his chief complaint.

It infuriated her. If she didn't get things done, who would?

These were the issues on the table when they sat down to talk to the mediator.

This was the next step on this road she hadn't asked to travel.

The mediation office was in Downtown Tampa, the firm of Fye and Forester.

The mediator wanted them to do counseling before they went to the official divorce route. He said they really could benefit from counseling, even if they ultimately divorced. He said it would help them have a successful divorce if they could establish clear communication. "Successful divorce" felt like an oxymoron, the jumbo shrimp of failure.

Jessie was willing to get marriage counseling. She was still stunned that Landon had left, even three months later. Landon did not want counseling. He was ready to get on with it.

"I don't understand why we can't see a counselor," she said for the fifth time.

"Because counseling isn't going to change the way I feel."

"Your feelings?" she said out loud. She didn't mean to sound bitter, but she knew it did. "It's the feelings for—what's her name, Kirstin?—,that I think are the biggest feelings we have to deal with."

"I am not dignifying that with an answer. I am not in love with Kirstin. And you know that. Stop with that."

"I mean, sure, you just up and leave, and Kirstin has nothing to do with it."

The mediator stepped in. "Look, you continue to argue, and we're not getting anywhere. If you both agree to six sessions, we can sit down and hammer out a separation or even divorce agreement."

Divorce.

She couldn't believe that was what was on the table now—but it was.

They went back and forth and in circles for another ten minutes, but finally, Landon relented. "I'll do the counselor, fine, yes, if it gets things moving along."

Yippee, she thought.

A marriage counselor—maybe that was all they needed. Maybe they could figure out a way back to one another with someone on their team, someone neutral. Maybe if they could talk and not bicker, they could remember each other. Landon used to think she was fun, but now she was stifling.

Am I?

They shared an icy elevator down to the parking structure. Landon finally spoke. "I'm not very hopeful about this whole counseling thing. It's just another thing we have to pay for," he said.

"True," she replied. "I'm willing to do half the number of sessions. Three sessions, and then we can call it a marriage."

He shrugged. No answer for that. For a second, he looked like he regretted something. Like he might soften to her. But the moment passed. She was back to business: "Remember, the girls need to be picked up at three o'clock."

"I know."

"Well, the last time—"

"Listen, I know. I don't need you to mother me."

"Fine."

"And when are you going to stop acting like a happily married wife on all your Instagram?"

"Oh well, for now that's what's paying the bills—or some of the bills."

"Don't start with me on that."

And there they were, about ready to get into a full-blown argument at the end of their mediation, during which they had agreed to go to counseling. It all seemed fairly hopeless.

They stopped mid-bicker and went their separate ways.

She got in the car, and as she put the seatbelt around her waist, she looked down.

She was too skinny now, she knew it. The stress of all this was eating away at her.

Jessie was stressed not because she was out of love with Landon, but because she was still in love with him. She didn't want to move on, or date, or whatever you were supposed to do. But she also didn't know how to change his mind. She blinked back tears. She wasn't going to beg him to come back. No fricking way.

She connected the seatbelt, put the car in gear, and headed out. She had one more haul to return so that she didn't get charged by Target for all the clothes she had posted about.

It seemed like every bit of the life she was sharing on her pages was make-believe. But maybe that's what social media was—make-believe.

As she drove, she felt a twinge in her side. What the heck now —indigestion? It stands to reason. My life is all stress, all the time.

Her phone rang. It was Mom.

She had to answer. It was just like her mother to separate from Daddy in the middle of Jessie's separation. Mother protested that Jessie was always the center of attention, but she was. Even this divorce was going to pale in comparison to Joetta's.

"Hi, honey."

"Hi."

"So do you need me at all for the kids this weekend?"

"No, it's Landon's weekend."

"Oh yeah, that's right. So, you have a little time."

Crap. It was a trap. Her mother knew it was Landon's weekend, and she'd walked right into it.

"Yeah, I guess so."

"I'd like you to come to The Sea Turtle. Anytime this weekend. I think it would mean a lot to me if you would meet your sisters."

The sisters—probably three unrelated women who were catfishing their mother. Another layer piled onto the layers.

"Mom, I don't want to meet these women that you believe are your daughters."

"Honey, I know I threw a lot at you and your sister the other day, but they are my daughters, just like you and Jamie are. Except I was a terrible mother to them, and I did my best with you."

She let that sink in.

So much of her life, Jessie had thought her mother was perfect. The house was perfect. Her society was perfect. The country club was perfect. Her mother's outfits were perfect. Her makeup was flawless. Her hair, always, well, perfect.

So much of Jessie's life was trying to live up to the standard her mother had set. To find out—even if it was completely made up—that her mother wasn't perfect was rocking her world.

She had talked to Jamie, and they had decided it probably was a good idea to get eyes on these three women who were swindling their mother. There was no way Jamie would be able to get home for this reconnaissance mission; it would be up to Jessie to see if Joetta was being swindled.

"Okay. What day do you want to do?"

"Saturday."

"Saturday is great. Let's meet at three, and then if all goes well, you can come to the Grand Finale."

"Yeah, but—the grand finale? What do you mean?"

"It's a lovely sunset cocktail at The Sea Turtle."

"Okay, Mom. See you Saturday."

They hung up.

The grand finale?

She'd be lucky if she could make it to intermission.

Fourteen

BLAIR

The area code was what did her in. She had lived in Cincy for ten years—she had friends, old business associates, even a vet that had that area code, so she picked up.

For a moment, it felt like a spam call; there was silence.

"Hello," she said.

Nothing.

And then there it was. There he was. "Don't hang up, I am calling because I know."

"What?"

"I know. Your ultrasound bill came here. I opened it, I'm sorry about that, but I did."

Blair's mouth was dry; she sat down at the little table in the efficiency kitchen. Blake knew. She had done everything she could think of to be sure he didn't know that she was pregnant. But he knew. One wrong address on one co-pay document, and her entire life was blown apart.

She wasn't sorry; she had actively tried to keep this information from Blake. He'd taken their breakup badly. He'd been controlling, lazy, dismissive, and eventually obsessed with her share of The Sea Turtle. All of it had culminated in an ugly scene that led her to get a personal protection order.

She didn't believe he was dangerous. Nor that he would ever hurt her. She did think that if she kept him away and out of her life, she had a shot at raising this baby on her own. Though lately, that idea was just as terrifying as dealing with Blake's temper.

She would have told him, maybe, eventually. She knew she had to. She'd also wanted it to be in her own time on her own terms. One form, one computer that didn't have her new address, had made the decision for her.

He knew.

"Are you there? Hello?" Blake said. His tone was soft; she hadn't heard a soft tone from him since before they'd moved in together.

He was always blustery, loud, bombastic, and then worse, angry.

"I'm in therapy. I wanted to tell you that. I understand that I've been too controlling. I've had a hard time with our breakup, and I've stepped over the line."

This time, she did have an answer. "Yes, you did, more than once."

," Blair remembered every time. She also remembered the feeling of powerlessness that had led her to the bar around the corner. And once she'd started drinking, she'd taken over the project of ruining her life, all on her own. Blake wasn't to blame for her alcoholism. That was a biological gift from her mother, or maybe even Bruce Kelly's grandfather? It was not Blake's to answer for; it was hers.

She was working on her confidence. Her AA meetings were helping. She needed to be the strong mother her sisters were. No Blake to handle anything. Just Blair.

Blair put her hand on her ever-growing belly and protectively rubbed it. She had a very important reason to be the woman she aspired to be when she was a girl, and that was the baby. As if the baby knew to answer, a little heel of a foot imprint slid across her tummy. For a second, she forgot that Blake was on the other end of the line, having called to—what? Apologize.

"I want to be a part of the baby's life; however, you'll have me."

"The PPO is still in place. There is no change," she said. She needed to be cold, analytical, and smart. She was the adult, and the little nugget depended on her. She was determined to put the best life in place for the nugget. Blake wasn't a part of that equation. Still, what was the legal side of this? She had no idea. Dads had rights, that much she knew. Split weekends and awkward drop-offs flashed in her mind, a future that seemed awful.

"I do not want to fight or upset you in any way. Your health and the baby's health are the most important things."

"Correct answer," she said.

"But—"

Here it came, the bullying, the ordering around, the Blake of it all.

"But I want to prove to you that I can be a good dad. That I can be reliable. I am so sorry for the way things went, and I will make this up to you and the baby."

"I'm done with this conversation," she said and was about to hit end on the call.

"I will do whatever it takes to earn your trust, I promise," Blake said. He'd never once said anything like that. He'd never once conceded an inch in their tug of war. And here he was apologizing, sounding gentle, being—dare she say—nice?

Her mouth was open in shock, she realized, but she also didn't have the wherewithal to answer back. She knew how to handle controlling and bossy Blake. But this Blake? She was floored.

And then the call ended, he'd hung up. No begging to see her, no insisting she tell him how much money the hotel had, no blaming her for his failings, none of it, just an apology and a promise.

Blair stood there for another moment. Was there something she needed to do? Was there a lawyer to call? Or did she just take this olive branch and move on?

Her phoned buzzed again; this time it was a text from her mother: Time to meet! We're on the beach.

Oh yeah, Blair thought. She'd nearly forgotten the actual emotional scene that she'd been gearing up for before her phone buzzed.

Blair was about to meet her half-sister; they were all about to.

She hoped that all this drama was okay for the nugget, because no matter what she did, drama seemed to follower her.

Darla looked at her through narrowed hazel eyes.

"Shh, don't tell anyone I'm chatting with Blake. It's just between us."

Fifteen

JOETTA
1986

She drank water or apple juice. She ate vegetables. She even ate lean meats. She took these awful horse pills known as Folic Acid. She took very slow walks every day, and she napped whenever she felt the slightest need.

Banks treated her like she was giving birth to the next monarch of England, like the cargo she carried was so precious she couldn't lift a finger to fold a sheet or wash a dish. The difference between this pregnancy and the three previous pregnancies was night and day.

Not that Bruce was mean, per se, when she was pregnant, but Bruce, via his mother, was of the mind that she wasn't sick, she was pregnant, and his mother and his mother's mother and all the way to Eve, women had done it. And they "pulled their weight."

They also died in childbirth; she wanted to tell them. But she didn't. A pregnant Kelly woman was expected to do just about the same thing as a non-pregnant one, i.e., every damn thing the house needed done.

And she did, as best as she could. She was a crappy housekeeper, a worse cook, and her ability to sew and mend was also at the bottom of the barrel.

When Joetta thought of her first three pregnancies, she thought of being tired and overworked, and afraid, and despite a burgeoning belly, she thought of that feeling, of not being enough, ever.

Her only fond memories of the chores required to have a baby with Bruce Kelly were the thrift shopping she did to find them clothes and cute things for their nursery.

It was such a contrast. She was now the Queen. Banks would have physically picked her up and carried her to another room if he found her kneeling in the bathroom, scrubbing the bowl. He'd already been treating her with kid gloves before they knew it was twins, and after, well, she could have rolled around on a down pillow carried by golf caddies from the club if she'd wanted to.

At first, it seemed like overkill, the fussing he did, until it didn't. At her height, a twin pregnancy was nearly comic. At seven months along, her belly looked like the same width as her height.

She had eschewed Banks' worries, most of the time, until this morning, when she was in the kitchen, grabbing a milk jug from the new refrigerator. The kitchen was so pretty, she marveled at how Banks had just let her decorate it the way she wanted to. It was all blue check wallpaper, floral border, and pretty matching honey oak cabinets. Not a whiff of the '70s kitchen she'd just left behind.

She involuntarily made a noise when the twinge of pain hit her side as she dropped the milk jug to the floor, liquid spilling all over the tile.

"Oh no," she'd said, and it was enough to have Banks come running.

"What? Are you okay?" Banks took her hand and then put a protective arm around her impossible waist.

"I just felt a little twinge; it's gone, it's okay." As she said it, another wave hit her. That wasn't okay. She knew what contractions felt like. It was too soon. This was too soon. There were stories she was telling, there were calendars that, if checked, would blow her life apart. Again. She willed her babies to stay put, not just for their health but for their future.

Stay put, little ones, just a little while longer.

"We're going to the hospital now."

"No, not the E.R., it's so crowded there, usually, and I don't want to do that. I'm sure it's okay." She tried to suppress a wince, but there it was again.

"Fine. We're going to Dr. Summers, now."

In short order, Banks had her in the doctor's office. Dr. Summers had somehow cleared his entire schedule, and there she was, the top priority. That was Banks, she knew it. That was money. That's what it bought: care, ease, security.

Dr. Summers had the situation in hand, and he'd done some sort of I.V. drip to slow things down, or stop them, or God knew. But Joetta was terrified. What she was able to convince Banks of worked because he wanted it to be true. Because he didn't understand how much of a liar she was. Banks trusted her.

He'd held her hand, spoken sweetly to her, and looked so worried at every moved Dr. Summers made. Finally, Dr. Summers asked Banks to leave.

"I'm going to need a moment with Mama here; you'll need to go out in the waiting room." Banks looked dubious.

"I don't want to leave her side. I can take it."

"Banks, it's woman stuff, seriously, give me a minute." Joetta winked at Banks and scooted him off like he was also a child. He shook his head, but no man in his right mind wanted to be in the room when any sort of actual female exam was underway. He kissed her on the forehead before going out the door.

"I'm going to be right out there, holler if you need me or anything changes, or we need to get her admitted or..."

"We're aware. There are a few magazines out there, find one and pretend to read it," Dr. Summers told Banks with a firm tone. Banks left, and then Dr. Summers closed the door.

He pulled the rolling stool from the corner, took a seat, and rolled to the side of the exam table.

He looked at the blood pressure monitor and then back at Joetta. "So, I don't want to get in your business, but you know whatever you say to me, well, that's just to me."

"What do you mean?"

"I mean, you're not the first momma to be that seems to be a tad bit farther along than the calendar would indicate."

Joetta knew that only her sister had the real facts. She intended for it to stay that way.

"It was just a little scare; you got me on track. No more contractions. We're good, right?"

"Sure, but I will tell you, not telling me the truth is a bad plan if you want good care. I'm seeing that you care very much about having a healthy pregnancy and babies."

Joetta felt a lump in her throat, and as she tried to swallow it, she burst out crying instead. No, no.

I have to keep it together.

"There, there, it's okay, you're okay, and I'm not saying a word. But let's get on the same side with this. How many weeks, really?"

"I'm five weeks farther than anyone knows."

"Ah, well, now we're getting it to it. Five weeks? Nothing to worry about whatsoever. Twin pregnancies often go early. I'll make sure Banks understands that, though I think we've got a few months yet, if you stay off your feet."

The kind look in Dr. Summer's eye made Joetta feel safe, made her think her secret was safe. And no matter what, it was the babies she was protecting, not the secret. She needed them to have a future that was secure. She needed them to be able to benefit from what Banks could afford.

"Off my feet?"

"Total bed rest. Whether you're seven months, eight months, or nine months, no moving around, and we'll cook those little biscuits so they're happy and healthy and ready for the country club. Got it?"

She nodded. Dr. Summers called for his nurse; she entered and started writing down his orders for her.

"And I don't think we have to worry about Dad out there making her do laundry, he'd carry her around on a silk pillow if I prescribed it."

Joetta laughed. It was going to be okay, just like she'd told Banks.

As the doctor headed for the door, she called out. "Dr. Summers?"

"Yes, my dear,"

"Thank you. I wish I had better words to use to say how much I appreciate what you've done."

"Shh. Nonsense. No more worrying, housework, or fretting. Doctor's orders."

She was going to hold this pregnancy at least four or five more weeks, and then Banks, and more importantly, her mother and his mother, would have zero to say about it.

Sixteen

JESSIE

She had been to The Sea Turtle before. She had a few memories of hanging out by the beach there, but all this time, her mother had told her that it was the hotel Aunt Didi and Uncle Jorge managed in their retirement. She had no idea that, in reality, Aunt Didi and Uncle Jorge were caretakers for this convoluted gift her mother had hidden. These women might be kind of dumb if they didn't know about it until now. Maybe that was it? More likely, as Jamie pointed out, this was some sort of grift. That was what she had to sniff out and report to her sister.

She wished so much that her sister were here with her. She was so proud of Jamie's service, her competency. Some days, all she could think about was that she was contributing nothing to the world, and her sister was giving everything. That had been the dynamic from as far back as she could remember.

Jamie, despite being her twin, couldn't be more different from her. Growing up, Jamie was the leader. Jamie was the athlete. Jamie was the one who spoke for both of them.

And now, in this situation, she was going to have to do the talking—because let's be honest, this had to be a scam. Her mother was the victim here, no doubt in her mind.

Their mother showed no signs of Alzheimer's or even being gullible. When the phone rang with a spam call, she blocked it. When an email came in, she knew how to check it. Their mother was savvy—especially for someone in her sixties—so these three women must be pretty good to make Joetta think this was her family. So they were either dumb relatives or smart strangers. Either way...

If her dad were involved, he'd put a stop to it. He apparently knew and had let this all happen. That's how she knew her mom's marriage was just as precarious right now as her own.

Their father hadn't spoken to Joetta in two weeks. Jessie had asked him about this story, and he said it was up to their mother to explain. He also wouldn't say why he was upset. He wouldn't put a date, a time, or a condition on when he and Mommy would get back together. He just said, *You need to talk with your mother—* which was pretty much what Jamie had said, too.

She was going to be the representative for the two of them in front of whatever she was about to face at The Sea Turtle.

She made one more call before heading to that beachside rendezvous, and that was to Aunt Didi—the fun aunt. They could call Aunt Didi for everything they didn't want to tell Mom about. They'd trusted her to teach them how to buy a tampon, to pick them up when they had one too many beers at a high school dance and didn't want Joetta to know, and they'd trusted her with their own secrets. Now it appeared Aunt Didi was the vault for bigger secrets than anything Jamie or Jessie could dream up.

She missed Aunt Didi, but understood why she was sitting out this particular episode of Armstrong Family Drama. Aunt Didi needed to rest and take care of herself. Whatever was going on here in Haven Beach was in no way, shape, or form restful.

"Hey, sweetie. I bet I know what you're calling about."

"Yeah. So I am going to go meet Mom and these three women."

"These three women have names. They're called the Kelly Sisters, collectively."

"The Kelly Sisters? Wonderful. That sounds like the Andrews Sisters. Were they popular in World War II?"

"'Don't Sit Under the Apple Tree.' Yeah, big hits. Look, I just hope you can have an open mind."

"What are you talking about? There's no logical explanation for this except Mom is being swindled, right? She's being swindled."

"Actually, no. Whatever your mother tells you is the truth. And you have to understand how much the lie has cost her over the last few decades."

"The lie?"

"Yeah. The lie. If you want to call me after you hear her out, you can. I can verify, or illuminate, or just listen—because I know this is a lot."

"Yeah. It's a lot. I mean...you're sure Mom doesn't have dementia?"

"Well, I'm not sure any of us doesn't have dementia. But the story of the Kelly Sisters is one you need to hear. And I'm just going to hope you forgive all of us. They had the most to forgive—and they have."

"Didi, when are you coming home? I hate to be that person, but when are you coming home?"

"We've got another two weeks on the Celebration by the Sea. Your uncle is now into salsa dancing, so it might even be longer than that. I don't want to discourage his burgeoning competitive dance career."

Jessie laughed. She missed Jorge. She missed Didi. She missed her own husband. Everything seemed so out of control right now. The pillars of her life were crumbling all around her.

"Promise me you'll have an open mind."

"Yes," she said. "I promise, Aunt Didi."

She was lying. Her mind was open only to the idea that this was bananas, and her mother was at the top of the bunch.

The call ended just in time to pull into the parking lot of the resort.

As she pulled in, the differences were obvious right away.

"Wow." It looked vaguely like she remembered, but somehow alive. In her memory, it was a dilapidated old place. This place oozed charm.

There was a new roof on the office. Roofers were working on the inn, next to the cottages. Jessie got out and walked the paths in between the two sections of the resort. The place was neat, but also artfully landscaped to feature the indigenous plant life of this beachy section of the Gulf.

Wow. Whatever the Kelly Sisters *are, they're*, they good at fixing up a property.

As she walked by the pool, she noticed gorgeous vintage tile, which was also an upgrade because that meant the water wasn't green. Jorge had been trying to make the algae go away for years, and poof! The pool looked cool and inviting.

There had been major upgrades here, which, of course, raised her hackles.

These upgrades were on her mother's dime.

Well, *that's* going to end right away, *if I have anything to say about it.*

The word *grifter* came into her head again. She tried not to get stuck there after her promise to Didi. But still, three adult women show up, and your mother gives them nearly a million dollars out of nowhere? Then your parents split, after decades of wedded bliss, all because of this stupid hotel? Wrong on all levels.

She knew her mother and Banks had a lot of money, but a million dollars extra for this? She wondered what the arrangement was. Would Banks and Joetta get some of the profits? Was it just a gift? She'd never even thought of her mother's money or her father's retirement. It wasn't her business. She wasn't someone hoping to inherit their life's work. Not in the slightest. She hoped they spent it on themselves. She hoped they made their Golden Years amazing. They didn't owe her anything. She didn't want them fleeced out of a fortune, however. These Kelly Sisters better step off if they thought they had found two hapless senior citizens. Jessie and Jamie would run them out of town on a rail if they were scamming Joetta and Banks!

On the other hand…,if her parents wanted to give money to Midwesterners who claimed to be relatives, what could she really do? Stop it? Probably nothing.

She had enough of her own problems to worry about besides her mother opening her checkbook.

As Jessie walked through the courtyard, she noticed how the cottages were all freshly painted, with each deck artfully arranged to match. There were cozy groupings of chairs, little white curtains blowing in the sea air. It was distractingly charming.

Wow. Whoever did this has quite a talent.

She continued to follow the path, and it led her to the beach. The gorgeous Haven Beach. For a moment, she forgot why she was even here. *Look at that sand!* She should take off her shoes and go running in the surf.

She was jerked out of her momentary seaside revelry by the reason for her visit. She spotted three women sitting at a beachside table, with the ocean as a backdrop. Her mother walked toward her, partially obscuring the three women. She wanted to get a look at them.

She felt nerves as she had never felt before.

Her mother filled her senses with concern, love, and her signature scent. Stronger even than the sea air. Joetta hugged her tight.

"Oh, honey, I'm so glad you're here."

Jessie hugged Joetta back, then looked deep into her eyes. Was there anything cloudy? Anything confused? Anything feverish?

The opposite was true. Her mother seemed calmer than she'd ever seen her.

No one would ever say Joetta was easygoing, but something—maybe the beach—had lifted a weight from her shoulders. Or maybe Jessie was projecting how, for a moment, the sea air had calmed her.

Who even knew what was true anymore?

"Come on. Let's meet the girls."

The girls. She and Jamie had always been the girls. And now *these* were *the* girls. Okay. Shoulders back.

Didi had told her to have an open mind. Didi had told her she could call afterward to see if any of it rang false.

And the moment Jessie came face-to-face with the Kelly Sisters was the moment she knew there were no lies.

"This is the oldest of my daughters," Joetta said. "Her name is Ali."

Ali stood up and smiled. She looked like she wanted to hug her but was smart enough to know this was delicate.

The thing that was clear as day was that Ali looked exactly like Joetta. Which meant Ali looked exactly like Jessie.

This woman was Joetta's daughter just as much as she was. The genetics were speaking loud and clear, at least with...what's her name? Ali. Ali was Joetta of a few years ago, and Jessie was another iteration. It was unsettling, this triad of little blond Joetta clones.

Another woman spoke up. She didn't look quite as much like Joetta; she had dark hair and was beautiful.

They were all beautiful, but this woman wasn't instantly recognizable as cut from the same cloth. She didn't look like Joetta or Jessie.

"Oh—hi. I'm Faye."

Jessie still didn't speak. What would she say?

And then the third woman, who was visibly pregnant, smiled at her. The third woman looked like a combination of the first two. A lot like Jamie, actually. That was equally strange. Jamie had a doppelganger, and so did she. They were all sitting at the table, and she was trying not to flip out.

"You look like my sister, Jamie," Jessie said, finally."

"Oh, thank you," the pregnant woman said. "My name is Blair."

"Why don't you have a seat?" Ali gestured to the chair pulled out for her at this little beachside summit.

They seemed welcoming. Open. But maybe that was the con. Maybe that was how they'd gotten her mother to open her purse.

She sat down and reminded herself to keep her guard up, even though it was painfully obvious she was at least related to Ali.

"I guess I'm the one who needs to kick this off," Joetta said. "These three daughters were born before you and Jamie. I'm their mother, and I was with them for the first ten years of their lives—well, ten years of Ali's."

Her lips were moving, spinning a fairy tale about her life before she had Jessie and Jamie. This was wrong. Joetta had graduated from high school and traveled the world, and when she'd come home, she'd fallen in love with Daddy. He'd been waiting for her all along. That was the story, that was the legend of Joetta and Banks. Not a teen pregnancy and a trip to some sort of midwestern hell scape!

Her mother paused and then continued to tell the story of her life before Jessie. "I am an alcoholic and have been sober since the moment I was forced to leave their lives. It is no excuse, but I was drunk and drove and crashed a car with their beautiful selves in it. They were little."

Jessie winced. She could imagine how it might feel to be responsible for a car wreck with your daughters in the back seat. It was unthinkable. Who was this person that Joetta was describing? It certainly wasn't the perfect mother Joetta was to her and Jamie.

"We're all fine," Ali said, putting out a hand to Joetta, who seemed to need it.

Ali was comforting HER mother. That was Jessie's job. What right did Ali have to reach out to Joetta?

"Well, I guess you can see now, Jessie, I'm a very good liar," Joetta sighed. "For your entire lives, I've lied to you, and I've lied to your dad. And if you want to know why your dad kicked me out, or why I had to leave him, it's because of this lie. It's pretty darn big."

There were almost more questions than Jessie could prioritize. What? When? Who else knew? What else have you lied about? None came out of her mouth except this one.

"But how could you leave your daughters?" asked Jamie. "I have daughters. I can't imagine anything that would tear me away from them." *That* was why this had to be a lie. No good mother could do what Joetta was claiming. And Joetta, though she could be annoying, was a good mother, a great one even.

Faye stepped in. "Our dad was a piece of work. He thought the only way to keep us safe was to cut Joetta out of our lives. So he did. And he told us she was dead."

"Oh my God."

Joetta was dead to her girls. How in the world?

"Yes," Blair said. "We thought we were motherless all this time. And out of nowhere, after our father died, we got our mother back."

Blair smiled. She was beautiful—so much like Jamie.

Looking at them was like looking at a family. A family she fit right into, at least on the surface.

"I don't know what to say."

"There's no right thing to say. God knows I haven't said or done the right things."

"Fine. Then I'm just going to be honest with you all." Jessie was stealing herself. She was trying to marshal the righteousness she'd felt when she walked into this meeting. It was evaporating, though, in the heat of this weird story. This weird, well, truth?

"Honest is a great idea," Ali said, giving a pointed look to Joetta, who smiled at the dark joke.

"Well, here it is then. I'm afraid the three of you are grifters, and you're trying to fleece my mother of her hard-earned money. Not to mention my father. You're clearly smart enough to know they have big money. I don't know what you've got going on from Toledo, but it seems to me you've hit the jackpot."

Joetta stepped in. "It's not a story. And they didn't ask for the money. I gave this resort to them long ago. It's always been theirs. But the repairs are more than they can manage. It wouldn't be a gift if it came with debt."

"Oh. How convenient," Jessie said. Still...there was no confusion in Joetta's voice. No doubt. Whatever *right mind* meant, Joetta was in it.

Faye spoke again. "This is a lot. Just like it took a lot for us to believe Joetta was alive."

Ali added, "And even more for me to forgive the past. But life is short. I've been missing my mother my entire life."

Tears sat behind Ali's eyes.

Jessie imagined not having a mother. She imagined her own daughters without her—to guide them, protect them, show them how to become women.

Her defenses softened.

Could this whole story be true?

"We're not trying to push this," Blair said. "We know this isn't normal or easy. We just want you to know...we want to get to know you. We're here if you want that. And we would never try to take advantage of her."

Jessie took a deep breath. Those words were good. She hoped they were true.

She was about to respond when a horrible pain shot through her entire body. It was so sharp she gasped out loud.

It felt like a little lightning storm in her bones.

Four women, strangers really, all keyed into her distress.
Oh no, not now, not in front of everyone....

Seventeen

JOETTA

For a moment, it looked like Jessie was going to pass out. Her Kelly daughters surged forward to help Jessie.

But it passed. Jessie's face had contorted, and her body clenched. She looked terrified. This terrified Joetta.

"Here, take a sip," Ali said gently to Jessie. Jessie drank slowly from the tall, cool glass.

Jessie drank slowly from the tall, cool glass. "I'm okay, this is just a little flare-up. I'm just a little burnt out right now. From other stuff on top of whatever this is," Jessie explained.

What was happening? She wondered anew about Jessie's gaunt face.

Ali wasn't a nurse, but boy, she was a caretaker. She found a cool cloth from somewhere and handed it to Jessie.

"I'm sorry, I'm a Florida native, which of course means I'm never outside," Jessie joked.

That was good, joking.

Ali was hawk-like in her gaze at Jessie. She wasn't satisfied that the trouble had passed.

"You know, this was a big moment. You're worried about your mom; we're all strangers to you. It's all a lot," Ali said.

Ali had knelt next to Jessie's chair. The two looked more like twins than Jessie and Jamie. That was another concern.

Joetta pushed that to the back of her mind. They were sisters, after all.

The tension lessened, and Jessie seemed okay.

And then Joetta's worries were sidelined a little again, watching her girls.

Ali, Blair, Faye, and Jessie together.

She was missing Jamie, but the idea that four of her five daughters could be in the same space and know the other existed seemed impossible, like something out of a dream she'd had over and over. A dream she had stopped trying to remember because it hurt so much when she woke up.

But there they were, tentatively talking to one another.

Jessie was clearly skeptical. She supposed her daughter had every right to be. Jessie looked at Ali, Faye, and Blair as grifters, maybe swindlers. Or she had until she met them. There was something so honest and natural about all three women that it would've been really hard to continue thinking they were bad seeds after meeting them.

Jessie had been disarmed, maybe by how nurturing the Kellys seemed to be. She was opening up a little.

She'd also begun to notice the actual resort. Though they were under construction, the improvements were extensive. It had been years of disrepair as Didi and Jorge got too old to manage the maintenance of the place.

"Well, whoever is doing the landscaping here ought to win an award," Jessie said. "The Sea Turtle has never looked better on that front."

Ali pointed to Faye.

"You're the landscaper?"

Faye answered, "Yeah. I'm part of the manual labor, ha. Actually, I sort of accidentally found a new career in floral design. Can you imagine? At my age?"

"Oh, you're THAT Faye's flowers. I follow you on Instagram. Your designs are beautiful," Jessie gushed.

One thing Jessie knew was social media, and apparently, the flowers Faye designed were making a big splash in the Tampa Bay area. Joetta felt a swell of pride for Faye.

She thought back to the flowers Faye used to pick in their garden—to the time, even then, when Bruce yelled at her for picking flowers. She pushed that thought out. It was so easy to take a good memory and pepper it with what went wrong or what wasn't picture-perfect. The key was holding on to those fleeting good moments.

And this was blossoming into a good moment.

She looked over at Blair. Blair was glowing. It was a cliché, but it was true. The longer Blair was in Florida, the more she seemed to become her true self. If Joetta had been an unnatural stay-at-home mom, it appeared Blair was going to thrive in the job.

Of course, everyone has a plan until the baby's up at three in the morning.

She chuckled to herself. She remembered being the mother of twins—how different it was. Even with help, there was never a moment to rest. But those newborn moments were such a blink of an eye. It was hard to tell any new mother that, but they really did pass so quickly, gone like a dandelion seed blown away on the wind.

The girls were answering Jessie's questions and didn't seem defensive, even though Jessie was clearly trying to be sure there was no scam.

Question one: "So my mother gave you nearly a million dollars. Can you see why I find that concerning?"

Ali nodded. "I can see why. I'd be just as worried. But your mother also gave us this property, which we never knew about. We didn't ask for it or wrangle it out of her. It was always ours, it seems."

"How is that possible? You had no idea you owned all this? Explain that to me again."

Joetta felt it was her moment to step in. "Well, I told you that through no fault of anyone else's but mine, I was a terrible mother to these three girls. I was drinking. And their father felt the only way they could stay safe was if I was out of their lives. Their father, Bruce, never told them. Didi took it upon herself to caretake it until they were ready."

Jessie's lips, which had been pursed when the conversation had started had softened.

Ali stepped forward. "I was pretty mad at your mom, at our mom, when I found out she was alive."

Jessie looked at Joetta. Joetta tried to sit up straight. Tried to own it. It was still hard. The worst parts of her life were lived in the memories carried by these three women.

Blair joined in. "Look, we understand this is completely unprecedented. But it's also something we didn't ask for. We didn't find your mom. We didn't know she existed. But after our dad died, there was a trail left at our house."

"When did your father die?" Jessie asked.

"Coincidentally, a few months ago," Blair said. "When we were closing up his house, we found your mom's, our mom's, clothes. Pictures. Things our dad never showed us or talked about after he told us she was gone." Blair paused then added quietly, "To us, she really was gone."

Jessie pressed on. "Okay. This is all strange. But once you found her and found out she had money—"

Joetta stepped in again. "I haven't defended these girls. I haven't helped them. I didn't raise them the way I raised you and Jamie. But I'm stepping in now. And it's always going to be too little, too late. I gave them this long ago. And I did it no-strings-attached. But there were strings, and it was up to me to make it right. Think of it this way, I'd have had to pay for the repairs if I'd retained ownership, either way. It was my debt to pay, in more ways than one."

She paused, trying to make Jessie see she wasn't addled or swindled or out of her mind. Maybe it was time to talk about rules, regulations, and the realities of running this place. Something they'd all learned a lot about in the last few weeks.

"You know all that legislation that passed in Florida after that condo collapse?"

"Well...sort of," Jessie said.

"We didn't do what needed to be done," Joetta continued, "because, well, you know Aunt Didi."

Jessie laughed. It was the first real smile she'd cracked. "Yeah," she said. "I do know Aunt Didi."

"I wasn't going to leave them with a gift that turned into an anchor," Joetta said. "I owe them. Even if they don't think I do."

Ali spoke again. "We're trying to figure out a way forward with a mother we never had. It's awkward. But we want you to know we didn't shake your mom down for money. We already owned this place. We just didn't know it."

Joetta added softly, "I gave this to them thirty-plus years ago. They've always owned it. There is no scam, just things coming home to roost after way too long."

"We're trying to make a go of it," Faye said. "We want this to be our business. And we'd love it if you were part of it."

Ali leaned forward. "This is split three ways—but if you say the word, we'll split it five ways."

Jessie's jaw dropped. "What do you mean by five ways?"

Ali smiled. "We're Kelly sisters, yes, but we're also daughters of Joetta Armstrong. And so are you and Jamie. If you want in, you're a fifth. And so is Jamie."

Jessie's look of skepticism turned to something else. Shock?

That was a real bombshell now, wasn't it? Three women trying to scam Joetta wouldn't offer to give up a piece of the pie.

It was a thought she hadn't even considered. The fact that these women wanted to share with their new sisters said more than any profession of innocence ever could.

It showed her, yet again, that Bruce Kelly, faults and all, had raised three women with a moral compass she could only marvel at.

Eighteen

BLAIR

The offer to share the ownership was sincere, but it was also one Blair didn't fully support. Her two sisters had convinced her. That said, she was in a different position, in life, and in her finances, than her two big sisters.

Her own nest egg had been smashed to bits by Blake's pie-in-the-sky business ideas. She didn't have a retirement like Faye or a house and divorce settlement like Ali. Blair's finances were on a knife-edge. Living rent-free in the cottage was how she was staying afloat right now.

Her sisters convinced her that they had to do it. They had to make the offer. Ali and Faye believed that the best way to convince Jamie and Jessie that they all wanted was to be true sisters was to open this business to them.

Jessie was rightly worried about all of it and had a healthy skepticism of the new Kelly branch of her family.

Who knew if they wanted to be a part of this, but on one point, Faye and Ali were correct. The offer helped relax Jessie. If they were scammers, they'd do no such thing. Jessie seemed to be coming at them with fewer accusatory questions and more purely curious ones.

Ali continued to be solicitous of Jessie.

As she did, Blair looked at her closely. The woman's color was very pale. Blair was the pregnant one, yet Jessie looked like she really needed a break. She could tell Jessie Jenkins was stretched very thin even before this family drama and the long-lost Kellys had landed in her little lap.

Even still, looking at Jessie was like looking at Ali about a decade ago. Clearly, Joetta's genes ran strong in those two.

They finished their little meeting, and it was nearly time for the Grand Finale. The sun, big and orange and spectacular, was about to put on its big show.

"We'd love you to stay," Ali said.

"I can't," Jessie told her. "I have to get my girls."

"That's right. I forget how much dropping off and picking up is required when they're young," Ali said. "Our kids are all grown up!"

"I mean, the hours I sat in soccer field parking lots, I could've written a novel in that time," Faye said.

"I generally work on my editing," Jessie said.

"I followed you, but no pics of your girls?" Blair asked. She really was dying to meet her new nieces, but it was a lot to take in for Jessie. She knew; she remembered the overwhelm when they'd met Joetta for the first time.

"I keep their faces off social," Jessie explained.

"That's smart," Blair said. She'd keep that in mind when she finally met the nugget.

Jessie seemed to consider something, and then she got her phone out. "Would you like to see them?" Jessie waved the phone.

"Are you kidding? Heck yes," Faye said.

Jessie opened her phone's picture app and showed them

photos of two sweethearts! One had flaxen hair, Joy, the other dark, June. It was almost like Faye's color.

"They're both in dance, and Girl Scouts, and Girls on the Run, and on and on," Jessie said with pride.

Jessie was a good mom, Blair had decided. She hoped this meant she'd have another person to lean on for advice when the time came.

"That's Landon. Sorry, my husband."

Hmmm, Blair thought," Jessie was *definitely* weird when she said that. What was the story there?

Joetta interrupted. "I'm going to leave you four. I need to make a run to Moe's. I promised to get the snacks for the Grand Finale." She hugged Jessie and left them alone.

Jessie waited until their mother was out of earshot. "I don't talk about it too much to Mom, but I am separated, currently, in mediation. She has enough weirdness with our dad right now, but that's my situation."

"I am currently separated from my baby daddy," Blair said and patted her growing tummy.

"I was a single mom, and this one just got divorced, so we're a real single gals club!" Faye said, and Ali shook her head in exasperation.

"Sorry, probably TMI from us," Ali apologized for her blurting sisters. She was the classy one, they always joked.

"I appreciate getting to know you, and your honesty. If we inherited mom's face, let's hope we didn't inherit her ability to concoct...whatever all this is," Jessie said.

And it was a lot, but it felt like they had connected, at least a little, with their new sister.

"And don't forget our offer," Ali added. "Talk to Jamie, see what you think. Someday, this will be a viable business, but Blair can show you the books. We're not there yet. And it may be a while."

Ali was serious. If it were a five-way split, they'd figure it out.

Blair was going to try not to worry about that anymore. She had other worries to fret over.

"Sure, thank you. That does help me feel better about Mom's investment."

Jessie had called it an investment instead of a scam, which was progress. A step in the right direction.

As they walked Jessie to her car, Ali took the lead, like the big sister she was. "I know this was all sprung on you; we know what that feels like. But we want to earn your trust. If you need anything, or need a beach break with your girls, or just anything, the Kelly Sisters are here for you. We are your family."

Jessie smiled and thanked them all. It wasn't an instant bond, but it was a warming of the initially chilly meeting.

Jessie drove away, and Blair looked at her two sisters.

"What do you think? She's gonna take two pieces of this pie?" Blair asked.

"That's not the way to think of it, and who knows? I think she had other things on her mind," Ali said.

"She's not well, that much is clear," Faye pointed out.

"She just got overheated," said Blair.

"That woman is overworked, underfed, stressed out, and is hiding something from the world. Trust me. I've learned how to see the signs," Ali told her.

"Well, hopefully we can help her when she's ready. Baby steps," Faye added.

"Right."

Blair felt at least part of that description could have applied to her. She was hiding things too. Blake for one, and her deep-seated fear that this whole venture couldn't survive them giving part of it to their new sisters.

Faye and Ali were better people: more open, more willing to wrap their arms around this idea.

But the worst part of Blair worried that she'd just gotten a mother in her life, and now there were two more sisters out there to take it away.

She knew this was irrational and probably her hormones talking.

Jessie was their sister—half-sister, at least—and they'd figure it out.

But it was one more complication in a very complicated life that Blair was trying to manage, without a drink in hand.

She patted her stomach.

"Girls, I'm going to skip the Grand Finale tonight. I am feeling tuckered out, too. It was a lot to process today."

Her sisters hugged her goodbye, and she headed back to her cottage.

She opened the door and collapsed on the couch. Sweet Darla curled up at her feet. Then Blair's phone buzzed; it was Blake.

She took the call.

After all, he was the father of her baby, and he knew now. There was no more lying to him. She'd have to figure out a way forward with two new sisters, one old boyfriend, and zero Pinot Grigio.

JESSIE

Saturday's meeting on Haven Beach was followed by a call on Sunday with Jamie.

"I just don't get a feeling like scammers," she recounted her impressions of the Kelly Sisters with her original sister.

"And they wanted us to take two-fifths ownership of The Sea Turtle? That sure doesn't seem like they're trying to get away with something. Unless it's on a sinkhole and they want to exact revenge on the sisters who had it too good," Jamie speculated.

"Pretty elaborate plan. I mean, I could be way off base. I don't have your instincts."

"I trust you. And your instincts are just fine. If you think they're not scamming Mom, that's good enough for me. I didn't find anything bad on any of them on my end."

"So no CIA file on them? Great, one less thing to worry about."

"What I am worried about is you. You're looking like crapola on the Gram." Jamie watched all of Jessie's content, even if it literally had nothing to do with her life. Jessie couldn't even imagine how silly it must seem, a Target Haul, when Jamie was doing such amazing work.

"Thanks ever so!"

"I'm serious. I realize Mom is an almond mom, but you, my dear, have gone too far. Eat something, okay."

"I am fine, but sure, yes. More food." Jessie didn't want to tell Jamie how fatigued she was, or about the weird old lady bruises on random parts of her body that she was covering up with makeup.

She had enough stress; she didn't want to worry her family on top of it.

"What's very weird is how much Ali looks like me, and we both look like the almond mom in question. And you look more like Blair's twin than I do."

"So, gene pool-wise, this all seems true. Wow. This is the strangest thing, thinking we have long-lost sisters."

"Yeah, tell me about it."

"Look, the other elephant in the room...do you have any interest in running a flea bag resort on Haven Beach?"

"Ha, it's not quite a flea bag, it's actually looking nice, but no. I have enough going on without washing sheets and towels for tourists and their kids."

"Okay, yeah, then nice offer, good faith. But no. Oh dang, I have to get going. Thanks for being the point person on this Joetta Drama. I will get the next one."

"Next one?"

"It's Joetta, you know, there will be a next one." Jessie laughed. Jessie laughed. "Love you, stay safe."

"Love you back, eat a sandwich."

They ended the call, and Jessie felt a little better about the Joetta situation; that was right before her own situation blew up in her face.

Although she had had a cold drink with her alleged long-lost sisters and felt slightly more at ease about the situation, it wasn't her only situation. In fact, it felt like the least fraught of the situations she was enmeshed in.

Jessie had to focus on her righting her own ship.

Landon's weekend turned into a Monday mess. This had become a pattern.

Her girls were at school; he'd done that right at least. But Landon had forgotten, well, everything. She was two hours away from the girls' school, returning a Pottery Barn Haul when the school called. Anytime her phone rang with the school on the other end, she had a cold, stark spike of panic in her chest.

But it wasn't a dire medical emergency on the other end. Just the standard, going-to-take-all-day-and-whatever-you-had-planned-to-do-you-can-forget-about-it kind of elementary school emergency.

"Mom, I need you to come to school."

"Why? Joy, are you okay?"

"I'm okay, but I forgot we are doing a presentation on Western migration in my social studies class. It's me, McKenzie, Bella, and the other McKenzie in my group."

Jessie tried to be patient as Joy listed all the participants in her group.

"Also, Braydon, he is in the group too and..."

"Joy, honey, can you remember why you called me?

"Oh, yeah, so I need a cowboy hat."

"A cowboy hat?" she asked.

"Yeah. I am representing a prospector traveling to California for gold."

Jessie blinked hard. What in the heck does a prospector looking for gold wear? And was it a cowboy hat?

"They wear cowboy hats?"

"Yeah. Mom, the presentation is in the last hour. Mrs. Crabtree said you should leave it in the office."

She should leave a cowboy hat in the office of the school before the end of her daughter's school day. Sure, great. Jessie did the math. That meant she had approximately twenty minutes to find a cowboy hat for her daughter, and less than ninety minutes to get to the school with said cowboy hat.

"No one else has a cowboy hat?"

"No, Mom. That was what I was supposed to bring."

"Okay. I'm on it. I'll do my best."

"Mom, I need it. I can't get an F." Joy was deathly afraid of failure; Jessie didn't need to hire a therapist to discern where she got that from.

"I love you; I will do my very best. I promise. Okay."

"Okay."

Jessie and her daughter hung up. All of the thoughts about her new sisters and the offer to take part ownership of The Sea Turtle flew out of her head, replaced with one question: *How do I find a cowboy hat at one o'clock on a Monday in Tampa?*

She wound up at Walmart, and there it was, of course. Everything was at Walmart. This one looked more Dallas Cowboy Cheerleader than prospector in the old west, but beggars couldn't be choosers. Who's to say there wasn't a cheerleader type on the Oregon Trail?

As she sped through the self-check-out, her appointment calendar pinged on her phone.

Doctor's Appointment.

The time flashed on her screen.

She would have to miss it. There was no way to do that and get the hat to school.

Jessie bought the hat and literally sprinted back to the car. The idea that her daughter hadn't told Landon on Sunday or her on Friday about this was a constant source of irritation in her house. There was always a project or a diorama or a poster board emergency.

If she had one bit of advice for any new mother, it wasn't about making the most of every moment or whether you should feed them a bottle or breast. It was to buy poster board immediately and keep it somewhere in your house, because you'll always need it, and it'll always be the middle of the night, or the night before the project is due.

Here she was again, racing along the highway with an item that her daughter desperately needed. Was this all kids or just hers? She suspected it was all kids, but lately it felt like all her problems.

She drove to the school, went to the office, and left the hat.

"This is for Mrs. Crabtree's class project. Fifth hour," she looked at her Apple Watch, "in fifteen minutes."

The school secretary gave her a disapproving look.

"I'm sorry. I just found out about this a little bit ago."

"Do you not check the weekly folder you get every Friday? It should've had that in it."

Jessie shook her head. "I did. I think. I did." She heard her own voice and didn't even believe herself. Landon had the girls on Friday. She could explain that to the school secretary, which would likely get her a whole new round of disapproval.

Had Landon looked at the high almighty weekly folder? She was sure not.

All of a sudden, she felt like she was the one about to fail fifth-grade social studies.

"Well, if you had checked it, you would've known."

"Thanks," she said, and the school secretary frowned at her. It was unmistakable that she was now in the running for worst mother in the fifth grade.

She could've gone to the classroom but decided it was best just to leave the hat. Going to the classroom would mean she'd have to talk to the teacher. She didn't want to talk to the teacher. She feared she'd get another disapproving lecture.

She knew things were fraying at the edges, but she hated to admit that it was impacting her kids. A year ago—two years ago—she would've been volunteering in the class. She would've seen all of the presentations. That just wasn't what her life looked like right now. Right now, it felt like a scramble.

She got back in the car and ran the mental list of things she needed to do before coming back to the school to pick up the girls.

Her calendar pinged and sent her a text alert.

Doctor's appointment. Overdue.

In the hustle to help her kids and return her haul, she'd missed her appointment. She had been so tired, and the bruises; she knew she needed to go. She'd call the office and reschedule; she did not look forward to the disapproval she'd get from *that* receptionist. It might even be worse than the school secretary.

She sat at the stoplight, looking at her phone, when all of a sudden, she heard a noise.

Oh my gosh.

The red light turned green, and she had been staring at her phone.

She waved her arms. "I'm going, I'm going," and started to drive. In that moment, a flash of a police car.

What now?

They clearly had her for something. She pulled into the closest parking lot, and the officer came up to her window and motioned for her to roll it down. Did he know she was the worst mother in the world? Was she being busted for not reading the folder? It felt like nothing she did was right, and now it was criminal, how bad at spinning all the plates she'd become.

"Ma'am."

"Yes?"

"Do you realize you have a broken brake light?"

"I do?"

When had that happened? Was it a crime? Sure, yeah, it's a crime. Of course it's a crime. And she knew it. It wasn't the first time someone stopped her. She'd just totally put it at the bottom of her to-do list.

"Yeah, you've got a broken taillight, and along with that, I saw you on your phone at the stoplight."

"I wasn't texting. I was just checking to make—"

"Ma'am, you are not supposed to be on your phone, looking at your phone, when you're behind the wheel. It's highly dangerous."

"Oh, I know. I'm sorry. It won't happen again."

"Let me run your plate."

She sat there. The officer had her license. She had the urge to look at her phone again and realized that would be a bad move.

After a few minutes, the officer came back.

"This is the second time we've stopped you in the last week. It looks like that taillight—you had a warning."

"I'm sorry. It's just—" she sputtered. There were a million excuses for why she hadn't done this or that.

"I'm sorry, but I'm going to have to write you a ticket."

"Sure. Great."

He handed her the ticket. "Now go get that light fixed. It's dangerous."

"Okay."

The officer's expression softened as he saw her eyes well up with tears. It just seemed like one more thing on top of a thousand things.

"I got it. Thanks."

The last thing on her list was a phone call to her doctor's office.

Before anything else happened, it was time to get the taillight fixed.

She pulled into her local service station and explained the situation. They told her there would be a wait, or she could leave the car there.

Leave the car there? She needed her car.

"I'll wait," she said.

She sat in the reception area of the auto repair shop. There was a TV on. She got out her phone again. At the very least, she could answer her emails.

She started answering emails, and then she got another alert on her phone.

What is this?

An email from Landon.

He didn't want to do the counseling, and he didn't want to continue to the mediation. He just wanted them to hash it out, between themselves.

He wanted want the divorce started? Now, no? Do not pass go, do not do the mediation, do not collect 200 dollars?

She wondered if Landon's work best friend, "stop calling her my work wife" Kirstin, was the reason. Was she hot to get him single a little faster?

It all made her sick. She felt flush; was she having a heart attack or something? She clicked the phone camera on to look at her face. Jessie was red, and her eyes looked sunken. She did indeed look as bad as she was feeling.

Her mind was racing when the mechanic came over.

"You're not gonna like this, lady, but the taillight isn't the only problem."

He proceeded to list things she had no idea about. Fluids, alignments, and on and on.

And somehow, some way, she snapped.

The car guy morphed into all guys, her guy, in particular.

"I am so sorry, but that seems like utter crap; it's all crap. I am trying to get back to school to pick up the kids, but I can't do that until this gets fixed and I have a doctor's appointment that I've put off for three months because I can't afford the time. It's like, three hours, do you have three hours? And every time I show up online I have to look perfect because someone like you says I need to smile more! If I smile more, my elevens show and my parenthesis and guess what, now I have a vagina neck. Thanks for that, internet. I have a couple of wrinkles, but now there is a name for it. What's the name for the food in your mustache? There isn't one. Why? Because no one cares if you have food in your mustache. Everyone cares that I have low collagen and high blood pressure, and I have done this to myself. Because I am supposed to be perfect, but there are no filters in real life. Maybe that's it, maybe I just walk around with a scarf over my face? Yeah, that's it!"

At some point in her rant, her heart rate shot up, and she started seeing spots.

She had lost complete touch with reality. All because they were trying to screw her over at the mechanic's shop.

She never blacked out, but it was sort of a haze. And before she knew it, there was an EMT talking to her. Did someone call the cops on her? Was she arrested?

She allowed an EMT to have her sit down in the back of the ambulance parked outside the garage. She was told to calm down.

She did, she breathed. She blinked her eyes a few times.

What the heck?

"Your blood pressure was dangerously high, ma'am. They called us."

"Oh, okay."

She pieced it together. She'd totally lost it. Like blacked out, lost it, but conscious. Lord. She was a mess!

"We'd like to take you to the hospital."

"No, no."

"You'll need to sign a form."

"Fine."

She signed. "I need to get going."

She'd need to go back in and apologize for her outburst. She'd need to get to the school to get the kids.

Jessie walked back into the reception area with her tail between her legs.

"Oh, look who's back. Karen."

She winced. She wasn't a Karen. In fact, she knew a lot of nice Karens. But she had lost her mind a bit.

"Can I just get my car?"

"It's going to be a few days."

"For a taillight?"

"And the alignment, and the fluids, and the tire pressure, not to mention the trouble."

"Fine. Do you know where my purse is?"

"Your stuff is here." He handed over her bag, and there was her phone. It was nearly out of juice.

She was late. The girls needed picking up now, and she was twenty minutes away. And she didn't have a car.

Landon was the last person she wanted to call, or her mother, or an Uber.

Tears began to well up in her eyes, and then a familiar face walked into the service station.

"Wow, you're twins?" said the mechanic.

"No, what?"

It was her brand-new sister, Ali.

"I think you need a ride," she said, "And I think you need a sister, and seeing as your actual twin is overseas, let it be me?"

"I just need an Uber."

"How about you let me drive you home, okay?"

Ali was acting as if she knew. How could she know that Jessie had gone bananas and nearly wound herself up into a stroke?

"I appreciate the ride, but my girls—"

"Joetta picked them up. You need a moment, or more. My car's out front."

"I appreciate it." Still, how did they know?

"And you, fix her brakes, fix her taillight, forget the rest of the list, or I'll call the BBB," Ali said to the mechanic, who'd suddenly gotten very quiet.

"Fine."

Jessie let Ali usher her out of the shop and to her waiting car.

"How did you know I needed a major assist?"

"You're live, did you not realize?"

"Live?"

"Here."

Ali handed her Ali's phone and opened Jessie's Instagram.

"I, what is this?"

There, in all her glory, was a meltdown on her page, in HD. Her phone was now dead, and she wasn't going to be able to immediately delete it. Worse. It was racking up views.

She saw that it had already been viewed one million times.

Jessie had no idea what it all meant. Had she accidentally hit the live button?

"I'll just take it down."

"About that...a customer posted another different view. Blair is a social media queen. She saw it and sent it to me. You need a sister squad, and we're it."

"Oh Lord, this is a mess."

Twenty

FAYE

Ali, in full big sister mode, was a sight to see.

And Ali was in full big sister mode.

Blair had seen the meltdown, live, on Jessie's Instagram. She'd immediately mobilized the Kelly Sisters, and they'd launched an immediate rescue operation.

"I'll get Joetta to get the girls," Faye had said and got on the phone to her.

Blair had handled explaining the situation to Ali, and Ali had practically flown to get to Jessie.

They had decided to hash things out at the beach. There was no better place, and it also meant Joetta could handle the girls without them hearing about the current crisis.

They were all now on the beach, watching the waves on the ocean and the waves of panic come over their brand-new sister.

"I mean, he won't take it down. What a complete jerk. I didn't yell at him; I just yelled near him," Jessie said, and she wasn't wrong. Two spectators and the mechanic's security camera all had different angles of her meltdown.

Joetta was managing Joy and June's homework and all the things that needed to be done for two little ones in elementary school.

The Joetta of their childhood could never have managed it, but today all they needed to do was ask, and Joetta was ready to go. Sure, she didn't have the speed or internet savvy of an Ali or a Blair, but pickup duty, she had that on point. Faye was both proud of her mother and slightly wistful of what might have been back when they were little.

Ali handed Jessie a glass of water.

"What I need is a good stiff drink."

"Not with that blood pressure," Ali said, and Jessie agreed.

"I'm just not used to making this much of a mess."

"It's fine, don't worry. Joetta is on it, we're on it, you can relax."

"So, I can't. This whole thing started because I am overwhelmed. I discovered my husband wants a divorce, like right now, and then the car, I missed a doctor's appointment, and well, I momentarily lost it."

"I've been there, trust me, I know. Caught my husband—uh, ex-husband—in the middle of his mid-life crisis and dumped potting soil in his red sports car," Ali told Jessie.

For that matter, Faye realized, all of them sitting there understood a man-prompted meltdown. One thing they seemed to have in common was heartache in the love department.

"My career as an influencer is toast," Jessie sighed. "Have you seen him calling me 'Taillight Karen?'"

Blair had called the mechanic, and he was getting so many views that there was no way he was taking the video down. He said it was a little free advertising for his business; men, sick of Karens, were all for taking her down and, in the process, booking appointments for oil changes.

"Would you accept some advice from an older version of you?" Ali asked.

"She's good, never steers us wrong," Faye chimed in.

"You need to go to that doctor's appointment, and you need to let your husband take the girls for a few days."

"But he doesn't know how to do the bows for their recital, and he always forgets what they like in their lunches and…"

"I'm going to interrupt you. I know you do it the best way, but you won't be able to do anything much longer if you stroke out," Ali said.

"If he's a decent dad but a crap husband," Faye suggested, "let him at least do the dad thing for a day or two while you pick up your basket and put the socks back in."

"What?"

"You need help, that's what we're trying to tell you. At least for a day or two," Ali said.

"I'd nag you too, Blair added, "but I'm sort of useless right now. Unless…"

Faye could see her wheels turning.

"Unless what?" Jessie asked.

"Unless you let me manage your comments and DMs. Let me deal with this for you so you can get to the doctor, get your car fixed, and get it slightly back on track."

Jessie seemed skeptical of all the help, but she also was clearly in need of it.

"And you can stay here, on the beach," Blair concluded. "I swear there is almost nothing that a few days of salt air and toes in the sand can't fix."

"It…I…" Jessie seemed to be struggling to be independent. To argue. To try to handle it all on her own, like she'd been doing.

"We've missed out on forty years of helping each other. Let us catch up," Ali said, reaching out a hand and putting it gently on Jessie's shoulder.

Jessie took a ragged breath. She said okay in a very quiet voice.

And then, she started to sob.

The three Kelly Sisters enveloped their newest member in a hug.

At that moment, they'd turned into Gulfside Girls, all four, just like Didi and Joetta before them.

Whatever Jessie had to face, she now had an army of three to help.

Twenty-One

BLAIR

Blair's mind was spinning on how to help Jessie. She had agreed to let Blair be her social media marketing guru until she got on her feet. This was Blair's wheelhouse, and she was excited to get started.

She was entering all of Jessie's login information, back in her cottage, when some messages popped up.

Blair looked at the messages. Blake. He was sweetness and light, and she was just glad this alert hadn't popped up while she was sitting with her sisters. They'd freak.

She also looked at her Venmo account. Somehow, Blake had decided it was his responsibility to help her pay for her medical appointments. She had crappy insurance, so she was paying a lot out of pocket. She hadn't asked Blake for that, but there he was.

She decided to call him.

"Hey, what is all this?"

"It's like—look, I just feel like it's my responsibility just as much as yours.

"Blake, I know your finances. You don't have the money."

"Well, I actually, that's what I want to tell you. I've got a new job."

"You've got a job? What about wanting to be your own boss?" She'd heard him go on and on about being a "disrupter" and about his "big ideas."

"Yeah, well, you were right."

"Wait, am I hearing this correctly? I was right?"

"You were. I need to work for benefits. I need to be gainfully employed. I need to stop with all these businesses. I really like my new firm. I'm able to work remotely if I want. There's a lot of opportunity and, well, the insurance package is really good."

The Blake that she first started to date, the Blake that she'd fallen in love with, was still there. Or at least a glimmer of him was.

"Yeah. I know you spent a lot of your money and time on my dreams, and now that you're, now that we are going to have a baby, I've realized that it's time for me to be responsible, to step up, to have a reliable income. Blair, you shouldn't have to do this alone."

"I'm not alone. I have my sisters, and if you remember, we have our own business."

She hadn't forgotten that Blake had tried to get his tentacles into The Sea Turtle. He, like Ali's husband, thought that the hotel was a golden goose, that they'd been stupid not to sell.

"Look, I know I have nothing to do with The Sea Turtle, and if that's your dream, you should have your dream. But that doesn't mean you have to cut me out of being a father."

"I'm not trying to cut you out."

"Well, okay, but you weren't gonna tell me, were you?"

"I don't know. I guess I would've told you eventually. In my time."

"I get it. You've got no reason to trust me. I promise you I have turned over a new leaf. I promise. I want to be a good dad. And more. If you'll let me."

Blair could scarcely believe what she was hearing.

"I don't think we are good together."

"We were," he said.

She tried to think back to when she first started dating him and what she thought about him and felt about him. It was all clouded by the end of their relationship. The end was when she'd been drinking too much, and he'd been taking all of her money to finance his dreams.

The Blake on the phone seemed to understand that all of that was wrong.

"I miss you, Blair. And I miss the future we might be able to build together. If you can forgive me."

"Forgive you? I thought I was the one who was supposed to be asking for forgiveness for my drinking."

"Yeah, well, I am not too proud to say that I probably am ninety-nine percent responsible for driving you to it."

Maybe it was the nugget influencing her, but in that moment, she softened. The idea that she could cut Blake out of this process completely seemed cruel. The baby she was carrying was made together. It was a part of both of them. If she hated her baby's daddy, did she hate part of her baby? That was unthinkable.

A kernel of hope was growing amidst the fears she had about forgiving Blake.

Was Blake the Blake that she left, or was Blake the Blake that she first fell in love with?

"I've got a lot to think about. I'm not sure about where I am with you right now."

"Listen, I'm coming down to Florida."

"What?"

"Yeah. I'm coming down to Florida. My new job is based there, kind of on purpose, to be totally honest."

"I feel overwhelmed with all this news, this change."

"Well, whatever happens, there is a baby, and I want to be part of the baby's life. And to do that, it looks like I've got to be somewhere near Haven Beach. And I need to keep doing the work to earn your trust."

"Okay." She realized that was a weak response; she didn't have the right words because she couldn't sort through her emotions this fast.

"And Blair, I'm going to do the work."

Twenty-Two

JESSIE

Her newfound sister army had managed everything from Joetta's annoying concern—and there was nothing Jessie hated more than causing her parents to fret over her—to dealing with the DMs that were flooding in.

She was grateful, overwhelmed, and still wary of the flood of family she was now neck deep in.

Her sisters had installed her in something called the Mango Mansion for a couple of nights while things were "sorted," as they said, with a British accent. She reasoned that it must be some sort of sister joke.

After a good night's sleep, Jessie sat in a surprisingly comfortable beach chair while a surfer-looking dude, who was apparently her half-nephew, by Faye, set up a cabana.

This beach seemed like a million miles away from her house; in fact, it was only thirty miles as the crow flies.

It was hard for her to sit down. To take things in. To stop looking at her phone. But right now, her phone was her enemy. It revealed that she'd screwed up, epically. Maybe it was always her enemy. Regardless of friend or foe phone, it was her job. Tough cookies if she didn't like it. It was her income.

Jessie felt a warm breeze catch the tendrils of her hair that had escaped her previously slicked back, perfect pony.

She had no phone to look at right now since the sisters had taken it to deal with her PR crisis. Why had she let them? She'd only just met them.

Jessie had no doubt Jamie would counsel her to continue to be on guard with this new family development.

Except...

They'd immediately offered to add Jessie and Jamie to the ownership of this place.

She looked around, reassessed a bit now that she had the time to just sit here, relax, and decompress.

The inn was in full construction mode. But she could see the vibe they were going for. It was so retro but not kitschy. It truly looked like Frank Sinatra could stroll down the stairs and head for the pool. There were no Disney characters, but there was a friendly vibe. She noticed a cartoon sea turtle on several signs that pointed to the pool, the laundry, or the cabana rentals.

She knew the only way her family had been able to do the full Disney vacation was because half of it was paid for by her brand deals. Jessie knew how much money families had to save to enjoy the happiest trip of their lives. Most would spend years saving for that week of fun.

As she looked around this place, she sensed what Ali was trying to do. They were creating a place where families could enjoy old Florida without taking a second mortgage on their houses.

Great idea, but could a business survive without getting the big money tourists in the door?

She had no clue about that one.

Meanwhile, the sound of the surf calmed her. She sank deeper into the chair.

It was odd having other people handle things for her. She was so used to managing all the details.

Her mind, free of the phone, wandered to the argument that severed her marriage. If she went back and honestly looked at her missteps, could she walk the right path in the future?

She opened the door of memory to the not-so-distant past when Landon walked out.

Jessie had been gone, taking back a Kohl's haul, and when she returned, she found Landon in the laundry room. She had staged the laundry room to perfection. It had the faux general store signs. She had a sign that read "clean" on the wall over the washer and dryer. Another sign read "detergent" over open shelving, lined with black wire baskets, and there was a sign on the door to indicate it was, in fact, the laundry room.

Landon was dumping detergent over a mound of clothes that appeared to be stuffed into the washing machine.

"What are you doing?" She scurried forward around him to look inside the washer. Ugh, he was ruining things. That was clear.

"What does it look like? Washing my gym clothes."

"Ugh, this sweater isn't supposed be in here, it will ruin. Did you even check the tags?" She was annoyed; he was creating work, not helping.

"It's not a cashmere ball gown or something, it's sweats, on normal setting. I think the universe will survive."

"You're not supposed to touch the hamper with the tan lid; that's all supposed to be washed a certain way."

"You're kidding me with this! I should have known—"

"You never know, that's the problem."

"I'm not trying to murder your clothes; I'm washing leggings, for crying out loud."

"No, you're making more work for me."

"I now need permission to do laundry. Is that where we're at? Of course it is."

"So Landon, you've screwed up, and now I'm the bad guy? Got it."

"I've screwed up? I can't wash my gym shorts without a permission slip."

"Stop being dramatic."

"Uh, I think that's you over there overreacting to me touching the dials of the washing machine."

"Could you just leave this to me. I will do it."

"Yep, sure can."

He dropped a handful of clothes on the floor, kicked them out of his way, and brushed past her.

She spent the next thirty minutes resorting and straightening the laundry room. She had content to shoot there the next day. She muttered under her breath. It had to look perfect.

Jessie almost didn't notice when Landon walked out to the car.

What is he up to now, she thought. He had his roller suitcase.

She rolled her eyes.

That was the last time he was in the house.

A seagull screeched and brought her back to the present moment. Jessie wiggled her toes into the warm sand a little further.

Laundry. She'd berated him for doing laundry.

Was he being too sensitive, or was she being too controlling?

Jessie knew the answer, but she feared she was facing it too late.

Twenty-Three

BLAIR

Blair was managing the multiple DMs, the emails from brands canceling their agreements, and the parody accounts making fun of Jessie's meltdown. She did not tell Jessie about any of it. She'd let a little time go by, let Jessie recover a bit, and then they could talk strategy together.

Blair watched a ton of Jessie's social media, going all the way back to lockdown.

She had to admit their sister was beautiful, and she could see why people followed her — to look like her, to know what she chose to wear, to know how to do their hair that way. All of her content was totally aspirational.

But as she watched social media, the cracks started to show. She could see Jessie becoming more brittle, doing things just for the viewers and not organically. It was a lesson, she realized, for someone like herself, who was a marketer. The key to successfully showing up on social media was to be yourself, and right now,

Jessie was the most stressed person Blair knew, except for maybe Blair herself.

She watched as Jessie tried to manage two children and a marriage that was collapsing. It gave her a sick feeling of fear in the pit of her stomach. Was she going to be in the same boat as a single mother? It almost seemed impossible.

The sun had set, and the guests had all dispersed. The day was winding down at The Sea Turtle when there was a light knock at her cottage door.

She peeked outside and saw Blake. She opened the door quickly. She didn't want her sisters to see, and thank goodness Ford was away on business. She had enough to manage without explaining Blake.

"Hey, just got in, and I wanted to see if I could do anything to help you out?"

She kept her distance, backing up into the cottage as he advanced slowly into the little kitchen.

But before she knew it, Blake was putting her groceries away.

And he did about fifteen little tasks for her, including putting together a crib. It was in the box in the second bedroom.

Could she have done it herself? Sure. But she had to admit it was nice to have help. Her sisters could have done it, yes, but they were busy with their own lives, and everyone assumed that the person who needed the most help was Jessie. Blake getting things done around her cottage while she worked on the problem of Jessie was a good division of her current to-do list.

And her sisters were correct; Jessie did need the most attention and help from the Kelly Sisters right now. She and the nugget were fine, and Jessie was in full meltdown mode, as the videos showed.

Jessie could continue her business as an influencer, but she'd have to change course. Blair typed her ideas, looked at the analytics of Jessie's accounts, and all the while Blake worked on things in her place, quietly. He didn't hover or insist she pay attention to him. That was also new. She appreciated that.

And then, as the night wore on, she was getting tired. She had fallen asleep on the couch. Blake, crib assembled, various light-bulbs changed, and a squeaky screen hinge oiled, came and sat by her on the couch. He was quiet. His words floated out of nowhere and into her brain.

"Blair, I was wrong," he said. "Blair, I was at fault. I was the one who should have taken the blame for my business."

He showed her that he was working, that he had a paycheck, that he had health insurance, all of the things that she was paying attention to more than ever.

He wanted to make it all up to her. He wanted to get back together. But he said she didn't have to answer right away.

Blake kissed her on the forehead. She also let him feel her tummy as a little foot karate kicked her from the inside.

Blake was saying all the right things to make sure she wouldn't be a single mother.

He left and didn't ask for more or push her to commit.

Blair also wouldn't tell her sisters one word of it. She made sure that Blake stayed out of the eyesight of her sisters. He agreed. He knew they didn't have a good impression of him at all.

The last thing she needed right now was to run the gauntlet of the Kellys.

She had to make this decision without their two cents.

* * *

Blair 2008

While her college roomies were cavorting in Cancun, Blair was home. She'd taken a few shifts at JoJo's Pizza, too.

"You will be making money, and they'll be making bad decisions." That was Bruce Kelly's word of wisdom when she whined about not getting a senior trip.

Her dad did not listen to the whining and went about his business at the plant. Most days, she slept in, popped over to TJ Maxx to hunt for some cute clothes to take back to school, and had even gotten a drink with her high school friends once or twice.

Still, it was no Cancun.

She was hanging out at home when the phone rang.

"Hello."

"Thank goodness you're home." It was Faye. Blair could hear the whir of machines and fans in the plant. Faye was at work.

"I am, sadly."

"No, listen, I'm so screwed. I need your help."

"Okay, what's up?"

"I was supposed to take the classroom snack and do this 'Read with Mom' thing for Sawyer, and I am not going to be able to come."

"What now?"

"We had three people call off, and I need the overtime, so I need to stay. Actually didn't have much choice, but whatever—can you go to Old Orchard Elementary with thirty-five cupcakes?"

"Wait, I have to make cupcakes?"

"No, just buy them at Kroger and take them over. The main thing is, Sawyer is on his own; he's going to be disappointed if no one shows." Faye sounded awful, like she'd murdered someone instead of just biffed it on the cupcake front.

"I'm on it. Just bring the cupcakes?"

"And they may have you read a book or something, but the cupcakes are key."

"Got it, when?"

"In half an hour."

"That's some last-minute shiz, sis."

"I really thought I could get out, but I just can't, so I panicked. I was going to ask Dad, but I forgot he has a union meeting."

"It's fine. I'll do it."

"Thank you so much. This would have sucked, especially since the 'Donuts with Dad' fiasco." Faye's voice was cracking. Faye was not a crier, usually, but clearly, she was in distress right now.

"I won't ask. Just remind me again of his teacher's name?"

"Mrs. Barth."

"Oh yeah, she's a stickler."

"She hates me, so yeah, let's go with Stickler."

"No one hates you. Go make the widgets. I'll be the favorite aunt for a day."

"Again, thank you. I owe you."

"Yeah, ya do!"

An hour later, Blair was trying not to swear out loud as she smashed her knees on the little snack table in her attempt to fold herself as small as possible to sit next to Sawyer.

Sawyer was about as cute as little dudes got.

"Thank you, Auntie! Mom never would have gotten the Funfetti ones!" Sawyer smashed a disturbing amount of cupcake into his mouth. She watched as the rest of the kindergarten class did the same.

"Glad you like them."

Mrs. Barth had looked at her with a nasty pinched face when she showed up with the goods.

"I thought Sawyer's mother was the one on the sign-up sheet. He is going to be incredibly disappointed she did not bother to attend."

Blair wanted to take a cupcake and shove it up Mrs. Barth's nose but did not bother. Her sister had been practically in tears at work over this ridiculous little snack time.

"This has become a pattern, I suppose it isn't a surprise," Mrs. Barth said as she led Blair to the snack area.

"What do you mean?"

"Children of broken homes are the ones to pay the price."

"Broken homes? This isn't 1956!" She couldn't help herself; this woman was too much.

"You don't have to tell me, that's the problem."

"Ah, how about I just sit with the kids then. Thanks."

Blair only had one parent; she wasn't that screwed up. A little screwed up, sure, but the way Mrs. Barth had it, a single parent was a nightmare scenario.

"Please tell your sister this is an unacceptable absence."

"Uh, she's not in the first grade. She's earning money to put a roof over Sawyer's head and keep him in Pokémon cards."

"Well, it appears Ali's the only one of the three of you who has broken the cycle."

"Cycle?"

"You heard me."

"I'm still in college."

Blair took a breath. This was not what she was there to do. She was there to be the fun aunt. She left Mrs. Barth to her narrow opinions and judgment and sat with Sawyer. Come to find out, he rolled with a stellar crew of five-year-olds who loved Funfetti, Pikachu, and Sponge Bob.

Mrs. Barth could suck it.

But Blair felt terrible for Faye if this was the environment and attitude she had to deal with when Blair knew full well that Faye was better than any dad or mom on this planet.

She grabbed a cupcake and took a bite.

She hoped there wouldn't be any left for Mrs. Barth.

Twenty-Four

JESSIE

Finally, with her mom and the Kelly Sisters dealing with all the other things, Jessie made it to the doctor's office.

She did the blood work. She did the physical exam, and she hoped that maybe they would give her an energy shot. Maybe she needed B12, maybe she needed to drink more water, maybe she needed to try to get more exercise. All of those things were probably true, but none of those things was what was actually wrong with her.

After the bloodwork was done, the office called. "We need you to come back in." They never needed you to come back in if everything was fine.

She was scared of whatever news she was about to get. She wished that Jamie were in town. Jessie didn't want to go alone. But she felt like she'd had enough favors. Everyone was doing too much for her. She did not want anyone to drop everything for her, again.

So instead, she called Daddy. "Daddy, would you come with me?"

"Of course," her father said. "I'll even drive you."

She remembered the carpet in the office, the picture of Dr. Singleton on a fishing boat, holding up a swordfish, and there was a bowl of mints. They looked as old as Dr. Singleton. Somehow, though, that was comforting; he'd been her doctor a long time.

Dr. Singleton shook her dad's hand and sat on the edge of his desk; he normally sat behind it.

Dr. Singleton told her the news. "You have what is called Acute Lymphoblastic Leukemia, ALL for short."

She didn't know what it meant. It didn't sound good. Acute equaled bad. Leukemia worse.

"This is very serious," her doctor said. "It's moving fast, Jessie. That's the tough news here."

And then her father stepped in. She wanted the doctor to talk, but Daddy wasn't going to listen to anything bad. This was fixable. That was her dad's motto.

"Well, we'll just get her the right medicine. What do we need? We'll find the right specialist. Whatever we need to do, we will do it. Don't worry, honey."

Dad didn't want her to worry; she had leukemia, but don't worry?

Dr. Singleton laid out the plan, and the bottom line was chemo and a transplant. He said it was curable, she could be okay, but it wasn't an easy road.

"What she's going to need is a bone marrow donation."

"Well, we'll be donors. We'll all be donors. I'll find a donor."." Her father wanted to fix it. That was her father. He was taking it worse than she was.

"Daddy, I'm sure it'll be fine. I feel fine."

"You don't look fine," he said. "You look tired. I'm going to get you a nanny. And our housekeeper." Her father was going to throw a staff of people at the problem; he'd decided it.

"I don't need a nanny. I want to spend time with the girls."

"Where's that husband of yours?"

"Well, that's kind of not something I want to talk about. I think my marriage is almost over."

"Oh, honey."

Her father opened his arms, and that was the best thing he could do. It was the thing she needed the most, a warm hug in the face of the cold as ice news.

Twenty-Five

JOETTA

She knew it was serious because Banks had not called her or texted her or reached out in any way in the weeks that she had been gone. Then her phone rang, and it was simple:

You need to meet me at our daughter's home.

That was it. That was the text. *She texted back, Is everything OK?*

No response. Just: *Meet me.*

It made her sick to her stomach to think what this could be, so she texted immediately to Jamie and Jessie:

Are you OK? Dad just sent me a scary text.

I'm OK. Meet you at the house.

So, her daughter was alive and hadn't died in a car crash or any of the million things that a mother thinks the minute something is delayed or a message comes through. In times past, Banks would have told her to be careful to drive if she was upset or not to drive at all, but those were times past. She was on her own; she was the one who'd left Banks after all.

She got to the house and found things looking a little different. Her daughter was a meticulous housekeeper. She kept everything neat as a pin, camera-ready.

There were dishes in the sink. There was laundry in the laundry tub. She decided right then that she would be spending more time with Jessie and help her now single daughter get through this time. Of course, her own life was also somewhat messy.

Banks was in the kitchen. He had no idea how to even brew a cup of coffee. She watched as Jessie did so for both her parents.

Banks looked older, sadder. She realized that life lately had taken a toll on all of them. Or maybe the consequences of her lies had taken a toll. She refused to let herself off the hook, even in her own mind.

"All right, you two, what's going on?"

Jessie pulled the stool from the island and asked her mother to sit down, indicating that Joetta should sit down.

"Tell me what's going on. I'm not going to sit. I'm not going to wait. What is happening?"

And then they told her. Banks took the lead this time.

"Our daughter has been diagnosed with ALL."

"What? What is ALL?"

"It's a blood cancer, Mom."

At that point, Joetta felt nausea bubble up from her stomach to her throat, but she realized it couldn't be her who was the drama; this wasn't about her. She swallowed the nausea and steeled herself for whatever Jessie wanted to say.

"A blood cancer? How did you get a blood cancer?" she asked. She tried not to let the rising panic affect her voice, but it did; she heard it.

"It's just something that happens, Mom," Jessie said.

"Is this why you've been so tired?"

"Yeah, I've lost weight. And why, well, I've got...well, stuff like this." Jessie took off her jean jacket. Jessie rolled up her sleeve. It shocked Joetta to see how thin her daughter had gotten. The worst part was that there was a huge bruise on her arm.

"Honey, what did you do?"

"I don't even know," Jessie said. "That's apparently one of the symptoms."

"Well, I don't understand. How far along are you? What's the treatment? We've got to get you immediately to a specialist."

At that point, Banks stepped in.

"I have called Dr. Watts. He's been a member of the club for over fifteen years. He's going to look at our girls' records, and we're going to come up with a plan. Don't you worry, honey."

Banks stood up and stepped forward, putting a kiss on Jessie's forehead. Jessie smiled and patted her father on the arm.

Her little girl was never more her little girl than in that moment, and Banks' strength seemed to radiate to both of them.

"Your dad is right. We'll get this solved. We'll take care of the girls. I'm going to clean your house, and Dad will get the right medical professionals on this in a heartbeat. Don't you worry."

"Sure, I'm not worried. I've got you both." And then their daughter, who had grown up independent, collapsed in their arms.

The three of them formed a tight circle of a hug. Whatever water was under the bridge didn't matter. What mattered right now was making sure Jessie was fine.

Joetta also needed to bring in one more soldier to this army. It was about time it got sorted.

* * *

She was going on seventy years old, and yet she was still worried about her babies. It was something that you never got over, that you never graduated from, that you never crossed a finish line from. Right now, it was Jessie she was worried about.

The dealership smelled like new leather and aggressive optimism. Joetta hated it. It was Banks who got the cars and just handed her the keys. She remembered now why.

She gripped the strap of her purse until her knuckles turned white.

She spotted Landon's office, a glass fishbowl in the corner of the showroom. He was sitting behind his desk, laughing into a phone receiver, leaning back in his chair with the easy confidence of a man whose biggest problem was hitting a monthly quota.

She adjusted her attitude. Jessie didn't need her mother to scream at her husband; Jessie needed her husband to wake up. She wasn't here to bomb out bridges. She was here to build them.

Joetta walked past the receptionist without stopping. She navigated the maze of cubicles, ignoring the "Can I help you, ma'am?" from a young man with a clipboard. She reached Landon's door and opened it.

Landon looked up, startled. His smile faltered, then vanished as he registered who it was. He said something quick into the phone and hung up.

"Joetta?" He stood, smoothing his tie, his eyes already darting to the door as if looking for an escape route. "Everything okay? I wasn't expecting you."

Joetta stepped inside and closed the door. Then, she reached over and twisted the wand on the blinds, shutting out the showroom floor.

"Sit down, Landon."

Her voice surprised her. It was low. Steady. It was the voice she used to use when Jessie was a toddler and scraped her knee. This Joetta was not the Joetta of Toledo or even the Joetta of Haven Beach. This Joetta was new. Burnished by years of successes and failures as a mother.

Landon sat slowly, confused. "Is this about Sunday? Because I told Jessie I'm swamped. She's going to have to do the weekend, and I'll pick up later in the week."

"It's not about Sunday." Joetta walked to the chair opposite his desk but didn't sit. She needed to stand. "It's Jessie."

Landon's face changed. The defensive mask slipped, revealing a flicker of genuine fear. "Is she hurt? The kids?"

"The kids are at school. They're safe." Joetta took a breath. The air in the office tasted like stale coffee. "Jessie is going to need you a lot now. And so will the girls."

Joetta looked at him, this boy she had known since he was twenty-three. He looked so young suddenly.

She softened her voice. "Jessie has cancer."

"What?"

"Acute Lymphoblastic Leukemia," Joetta said. She forced herself to say the words clearly, even though they felt like gravel in her throat. "ALL. She's been diagnosed with it. It's aggressive but curable, but we're going to have to fight it with her."

Landon stared at her, his mouth opening and closing. "Leukemia? But...she's young. She just...she was just tired. She said she was tired."

"She is very sick, Landon." Joetta moved around the desk. She placed her hands on his shoulders, feeling the tension in his suit jacket.

"Oh my god. Jessie."

He started to crumble. Joetta saw the knees buckle, saw the sob rising in his throat. He was going to fall apart.

No, she thought fiercely. *You do not get to fall apart. Not yet.*

"Landon, look at me." She gave his shoulders a sharp squeeze. "Look at me."

He lifted his head, his face wet.

"I know you're scared," she said. "I know this is a nightmare. But right now, whatever stupid crap is keeping you away, that's over. That's petty. This is real, and it is time to forget about that and get in the game with her."

Landon let out a choked sound, burying his face in his hands.

"I don't care what the problem is or was; this is bigger," Joetta said. "None of that matters. The slate is clean. What we do now is what we have always done when Jessie needed us. Got it?"

She waited until he lowered his hands.

"I don't know if I can," he whispered. "I'm not...I'm not strong like you, Joetta."

Joetta almost laughed. *Strong?* She felt like she was made of glass most of the time. But maybe she was strong. He was, too. She knew he'd find the man he wanted to be. The one Jessie needed.

"We are all going to be strong, we're going to be whatever she wants. Got it?"

Landon took a shuddering breath. He looked at the framed photo on his desk. Jessie and the girls all dressed up on Easter Sunday.

"Okay," he whispered. He wiped his eyes with the back of his hand.

"Take a leave here if you need to, but you're the point person on this. Starting now. The man I know you are is in there."

Landon grabbed his keys. He didn't look at his phone. He didn't look at the invoices. He looked at the door.

"I'm going," he said.

"Good." Joetta watched him go. She watched him run out of the office, ignoring the sales manager who tried to flag him down.

When the door closed behind him, Joetta finally let herself sink into the chair he had vacated. She put her head on the cool, polished mahogany of the desk.

Phew, that worked. She knew all he needed was a push, but it was a massive relief that it was just a little nudge in the direction of getting Jessie all the support she deserved.

Twenty-Six

BLAIR

When Blair approached the cottage, she knew right away something was wrong. Something was different. Joetta Armstrong was one of the most determined people she had seen in the last few years, rivaled only by maybe Ali. She opened the cottage door.

"You look like you've had a rough day. What's wrong?"

"Oh, honey, I have had a rough day, but it's not about me. Could you get Ali and maybe Faye on the phone?"

"Sure. Are you okay?"

"I'm okay, but Jessie isn't."

A short hour later, all three Kelly sisters took in the information and created a plan. Ali was nothing if not organized, and Joetta was happy to have the three girls help her with Jessie's life.

"I'm on the list to pick up the girls from school," Joetta said.

"Let's get the three of us on the list too, so that the aunties can do what aunties do," Faye suggested. That was key; any one of them might need to pinch hit for their little nieces.

Blair wondered how she would handle additional things on

top of what she was juggling, like being an auntie to two littles going through such a scary thing. But they'd adjust, little ones adjusted.

She really hoped her little nieces would like to help her with her little nugget. That was a fun thing to look forward to in all the scary news that they were now managing.

"Okay, that's step one. Step two is her business. Blair, you have some ideas, don't you?" Ali was planning, marshalling, handling every component like the field general she was.

"I do have some ideas, but I don't know that she's ready for them. If Jessie lets me, I'm going to repost a lot of her content. She doesn't seem to have really maximized her most popular videos. That'll buy us plenty of time while she's still got engagement and followers, and she's earning money but doesn't have to shoot anything or do anything whatsoever."

"Oh, that sounds like a wonderful idea," Joetta said.

Blair's mind raced with ideas of how to make sure Jessie didn't have to worry at all about her influencer business.

Ali piped up, "What about housework?"

"Our housekeeper is family," Joetta explained. "Jessie has said no in the past, but I think maybe that's the play? Someone who she already knows and loves."

"Well, we've got to let her take the lead," Ali said, "but one thing we know for sure is that she's going to need space, time, and good food."

"Ha, ha! That's it. I'm going to start a food train. She is dangerously thin," Faye said.

"Well, we'll figure out what she likes. We'll figure out what tastes good. We'll take care of the things she doesn't want to. Or doesn't have energy for," Ali said.

"What she's going to want is to spend time with her girls," Joetta pointed out.

"That's her for sure."

The three sisters worked with Joetta to come up with a plan of attack. They couldn't fight ALL, but they could make sure that any moment Jessie had was devoted to her girls and her health.

There was one more thing Joetta hadn't thought of quite yet.

Blair piped up, "What I'm looking at here is the treatment. What are they saying they want to do for her?"

"Well, Banks's friend, Dr. Walls, is looking at all of her lab work to see what the best course of action is."

"All right. Well, whatever it is—she needs a kidney, she needs an extra arm—whatever it is, we've got plenty," Blair said.

Joetta smiled, but it wasn't an easy one. Blair ached for their mother just as much as she did for Jessie.

<h1 style="text-align:center;font-style:italic">Twenty-Seven</h1>

BLAIR
2003

Blair straightened the satin of her dress. She'd chosen a deep purple from Chache. She had a little crocheted sweater on top because it was freezing.

Her platform sandals were so cute, but she was pretty sure she was going to lose a toe to frostbite. She didn't care. It looked cute.

Her hair, straightened to within an inch of its life, was holding, for now. But if they didn't walk out on the field soon, it would puff up beyond all recognition.

Where *is* he?

Her dad was supposed to walk her out on the field during halftime. She'd told him the time a million times. He was proud of her; she knew he was, even if he hadn't said much.

"Well, don't get your hopes up," he'd said. "Your sister was also on the court, if I remember, and she got a paper crown from Burger King."

This was wrong. Ali got an actual tiara. Blair absolutely knew this because she'd played dress up with it from the moment it got into their house.

Whatever, she just needed Bruce to walk her on the field, and then she'd change, go to the bonfire, and have actual fun. This part was kind of nerve-racking. The girls on the court would be announced, they'd walk down the field with their parents, and then boom, the announcement.

She didn't figure she'd win. Ali was the nicest person on the planet; everyone at the school still said it. She'd been there a million years ago, but all the teachers remembered her. Blair wasn't as pretty or as nice, but she did have a good sense of humor, and she had a wide range of friends, which was how she'd got picked at all, she thought.

Blair tried not to look at the other four girls on the court. They were all standing with their moms and dads. She only had Bruce, but maybe that was also how she'd got votes. No mom, aw, so sad.

She wasn't really sad about it since she couldn't miss what she never had, but dang, she sure did wish Bruce would get there.

Mrs. Dunn came up to her. "Honey, I don't want to be mean, but we can't wait for your dad; half time is half time, and they can't change the time or the team gets penalized."

"I'm sure he's on the way." She said it confidently, but inside, she was freaking out.

What if he didn't show? Would they let her walk by herself?

That would be so fricking embarrassing. She'd also probably trip over her platform sandals with her frozen toes.

"Girls, line up. Blair, you go last, just in case."

The other girls filed in front of her.

Kelly San Giles edged in front of her.

Her parents are earning.

"Are you sure you don't want to sit this out? You're supposed to have an escort." It was said in a sickly-sweet way. Her parents probably thought she was being nice. But Blair saw the look in the girl's eye. She was enjoying Blair's misery.

Why were some people so mean?

They started announcing...

"Now it's time to meet the Start High School Homecoming Court!" The announcer's voice boomed, filling the air.

Soon, very soon, they were going to say her name, and she'd be all alone.

The court filed out one by one.

Still no Dad.

Blair saw two people running toward her. What the heck?

She blinked. There were Ali and Faye!

They made it to both sides of Blair.

"What's going on? It's supposed to be Daddy."

"We know, we know. He's at work, extra shift," Faye explained.

Sometimes, Blair hated that factory. How in the world could Faye stand to work there?

"Why didn't he say no? He knew I had this?"

"You know Dad, work, work, work," Faye said.

Blair blinked away tears. Why couldn't she just have at least one parent? The rest of the girls had two. She was feeling like crawling into a hole and dying.

Ali put an arm through hers.

"Don't you dare cry. We spent hours getting that makeup right. Now stand up straight, we're walking ya."

It was as bracing as a slap in the face. Ali was nice to the world, but to her family, she was a can-do, get-it-done, stiff upper lip, boss babe. There was no arguing in that moment.

Blair did as she was instructed, and the three Kelly Sisters marched out on that field as a unit.

She did not win, but at least she didn't lose alone.

Twenty-Eight

JOETTA
Present Day

It was her last lie. It was the one she'd had help to keep from Didi and from the doctor. But it was the doctor's words today that would reveal the truth.

They were hearing about Jessie's treatment plan. They always tried to have someone with Jessie at her appointments, ready to take notes or ask follow-up questions. Whatever she needed. When it came to medical information, it was always good to have several sets of ears, she'd learned. But this one, this big one, Jessie wanted to do it alone.

Joetta had waited in the waiting room and driven her daughter to the club, where all three would sit together and take whatever medicine Jessie had to dish out.

Joetta and Jessie had gone from the latest doctor's appointment to Banks' club in near silence. They'd walked through the club to Banks' office. Banks had arranged for sandwiches for all three in the office's well-appointed sitting area.

Joetta looked around. It was decorated to impress, this place.

She'd done it. She'd made sure Banks looked the way an important man should; she'd selected the paint, carpet, and furnishings all here to convey the same. She had enjoyed many meals with him in this space when he had to work late or nightcaps after the club had finished hosting an affair.

But now, it was the three of them; Jamie was also set to call in, so they could keep her in the loop.

Jessie's phone buzzed, and there she was, Jamie, on FaceTime.

Joetta felt a physical ping, seeing Jamie. She recognized it as the frayed nerve ending that throbbed and ached anytime she was away from her girls. The one she'd lived with for thirty years. In the last few months, she almost didn't feel it. The Kelly Sisters had changed her life in that regard. That omnipresent lack of them was filled!

But seeing Jamie was a harsh reminder; it was all so tenuous. Would she pay for her sins by losing daughters when she gained others?

Didi would tell her this was an awful and ridiculously superstitious way to live. She'd tell her to stop it.

Joetta tried to lean into the grateful energy that Didi always had.

"Sis, hello!" Jamie said from the screen. "How are you doing?"

"I'm okay, I just got the plan from the doctors, and I thought I'd share it with you guys. Because, well, you'll see."

"Yes, for sure."

Jessie positioned her phone so they could all see Jamie.

"Hi, Bug," Banks said and blew her a kiss.

Joetta gave a small wave. She didn't know if she could speak. Jessie wanted to tell them when they were all together. So she wouldn't have to go through it over and over.

"Okay, it's as we suspected, it is ALL, totally, but the plan is very aggressive."

Joetta felt the words like a punch in the gut.

"I'm going to go forward, okay. I know that was tough, Mom, but I can't stop."

"Go on," Banks said.

He was right. Her daughter shouldn't have to worry about them; it should be all about her, not them.

"I do not want to sugarcoat it. This could kill me, but it doesn't have to."

Joetta wanted to scream, cry, and punch something. Instead, she said something inane.

"We don't have this in the family. They can't be right."

"Mom, it is right. It's the diagnosis. I've had all the second opinions. Dad's doctor buddy made sure I had every test needed."

"What's the treatment?" Jamie asked—Jamie, always the planner, the practical one. The doer.

She was right, there was a treatment, they'd get it for her, immediately. The best of whatever she needed. Joetta was about to bargain with the Lord above for whatever she could think of to make sure Jessie was okay.

"They are going to do chemo, but also, because this has moved fast and come out of nowhere, they're going to want to do a bone marrow transplant."

"I'm in, where do I get tested?" Jamie said.

"Thank you, sis. We're fraternal twins, so it might not be a match, but there's a good chance."

"Let me get tested first," Banks said. "You're overseas; we can test me immediately."

Joetta's mind woke up to what he was saying. What it meant to the last lie she had told.

"There are eight markers, and if we can get all eight, I have the most success of beating this," Jessie said.

Joetta was reeling, and now, before they moved any further, she knew it was time to end the lie. Her daughter's life depended on it.

"No, Banks, do not waste time, we can't afford to," Joetta said.

Her family looked at her like she was stupid. Like she didn't understand what Jessie had explained.

"I'm sure it's not a waste of time," Banks replied, confused. "If I'm not a match, we'll get Jamie in the pipeline. And you."

"That sounds good, Dad," Jessie said.

"No, I mean, you're all about to hate me even more than you do now. But we can't waste time testing you because…"

"Joetta swallowed hard, it was right there, in her throat, the truth that would crush any chance of happiness or reconciliation with Banks. But it didn't matter.

Nothing was as important as quickly finding a donor for Jessie.

She barreled forward and spilled it all.

"You're not the biological father of Jamie and Jessie," Joetta said. Banks looked at her, and she had no idea what he was thinking. He was like a statue.

"Mom, what now, really? With Jessie sick? You have got to be kidding, trying to get attention now!"

"Jamie was angry. No ocean in between them could disguise it. Her words hurt, but Joetta figured they were the first of more anger to come, as they processed her latest, biggest lie.

"I wish you were their father, and you are, you were, but I was pregnant with the girls when we met."

"Jeez, Mom, seems like everything you say is a lie," Jessie said and rubbed her eyebrows with her fingers.

She was so skinny. Joetta saw another bruise on her forearm, a symptom of the disease, she knew.

She winced at the insult but understood it; she deserved it all. But she would take it. They could disown her, kick her to the curb. Revealing this lie might destroy her life, but it damn well wouldn't kill her daughter by wasting time testing Banks.

"I am telling you now, we don't have time to waste. We need Jamie tested, and me," Joetta said.

Banks hadn't said anything yet, but he walked toward Jessie and put his arms around her.

"You're my daughter, you both are, thicker than blood. But really, this is good news."

"What?" Jessie asked.

And Joetta wondered the same thing: What in the world was good about any of this?

"The Kelly Sisters are full-blood sisters of our girls? That's what you're saying, right?"

"Yes," Joetta said.

"Well, then you have four chances plus Mom. We'll get this match exact. See, it's good news."

Banks then walked over to Joetta, his eyes seemed softer. Or was she now just hallucinating?

"I'm glad you finally told me. That had to be hard," he said.

And there was the old Banks, the one who believed in her. He reached out a hand and held it in hers.

She wanted to sob, to collapse in his arms. But again, it felt wrong; her marriage was beside the point now. The point was Jessie, and being honest enough to do everything she could to get her better.

"You two are bananas, I mean, really totally bananas," Jessie said.

"Yeah, what the hell, Mom?" Jamie added. "Really, what the hell?"

"Let's focus on Jessie; you can hate me later," Joetta told her.

"They don't hate you; we all love you, and we all need to get Jessie better, agreed?" Banks said.

"Agreed," Jamie said.

Joetta did cry now, softly, into the shoulder of the love of her life, and the true father, if not the biological one, of her beloved twins.

Twenty-Nine

BLAIR

Much of her job was numbers. Or rather, data. What age range were their posts hitting? Were the things she was sharing finding people who would vacation at the resort? What type of posts did the big resorts put out there? Who did they target?

Blair spent hours and hours analyzing the numbers, trends, and bar graphs to see exactly how to target the people who would book The Sea Turtle Resort.

She also looked at the types of posts that did well on their Facebook, Instagram, and TikTok accounts. She'd been the one who'd started them all. The difference between being a part owner of The Sea Turtle and working for her marketing firm was that not only did she have to analyze, but she also had to create the actual content.

That meant telling the story of The Sea Turtle was up to her. At her old job, she interpreted the data and told the social team what worked and what didn't. They'd go get the photos she needed or edit the videos. They'd post and monitor and share, and she'd look under the hood and help the clients refine the messaging. Now she was the entire team.

She had Sawyer helping Faye with content on Faye's floral arranging business, but for The Sea Turtle, it was all hers. Ali was an organizational whiz, a managerial master, and a great boss, but give her a camera and you'd get a dozen blurry photos of an off-kilter sunset.

Not to mention, Ali was busy. Blair watched her big sister manage everything and knew if they were going to get the resort bookings they needed, it would be up to her to tell the stories and get the word out to snowbirds looking for a beautiful but affordable slice of an old Florida vacation.

Which is precisely how she'd found herself lying on the sand, trying to get a turtle's eye view of the resort. She figured if she couldn't donate blood or whatever Jessie needed, she could be the best darn marketing professional this resort and Jessie's personal brand could ever want! Go marketing! She laughed at herself, but in fact, if they didn't book rooms, all of this was going to go away.

"Is that good for the baby?" It was Blake, again, showing up out of nowhere, and slightly hovering.

"You startled me," Blair said. "I would have jumped a foot, you startled me. Problem is, I can only roll over and attempt to lumber back to a standing position."

"Sorry to startle you. Can I ask what you're doing down there? You scared me when I looked out here and saw you, uh, like that."

"Yeah, well, it's for a social media series I'm doing for the resort, a turtle's eye view is the concept."

"I get it, I like it. Have the turtle with a margarita, have the turtle on a paddleboard, really living up the beach life."

Blair looked at Blake and was reminded that he was creative when he wanted to be. He'd just gotten it in his head that he needed to be a tech bro or a boss.

"Two ideas I hadn't thought of, I like it. I'd write it down, but well..." Blair struggled to roll to some sort of upright position. The bump was getting bigger by the second, and she was surprised to find out that she'd become significantly less mobile over the last few days. Well, less agile, at least.

"Here." Blake put his hand out, and she gratefully took it. She was now in a reasonable sitting position.

"Okay, that's better. I'm trying to get the resort, like the cabana area, in the background."

"I see the vision, may I?" He gestured for her to give him the camera, so she did.

Blake crouched down to turtle eye view and took a few shots and a few videos.

Her phone buzzed while he had it.

Oh no. He'd been so controlling before, every text monitored, every friend screened by him.

Whoever was texting her was likely going to lead to the third degree inquiry. She braced herself to defend her life, her privacy, like she was used to doing with him.

"Here, you're getting a text." Blake handed her the phone, without quizzing her on who it was or why they wanted to text her.

She looked at the phone; it was from Faye, about Joetta wanting to meet with them, and whether they were all going to be at the Grand Finale tonight.

She thought she'd push it a little more, test Blake's seemingly nonchalant attitude about her incoming messages. She responded to the text and smiled to herself, just for an extra bit of pressure.

Blake didn't take the bait. He looked out at the surf and waited patiently while she sent her reply.

"Okay, so, look at the photos, are we realizing the vision?"

She opened her camera roll. "Actually, yes, this is great, ooh, this one too." She scrolled through.

"Excellent, glad to help. So...I had a question for you."

"You didn't show up just to take turtle photos?"

"I can, or would, all you have to do is ask. But no, the question is about childbirth classes."

"What about them?"

"I assume you'd probably have a line out the door for people to go with you, but I am the father, and I would be honored."

Blair was taken aback. She blurted the honest truth to Blake, no more tests or sly hoops to jump through.

"You are technically not supposed to be within 100 feet of me after that stunt you pulled!"

"About that...I am eternally regretting that. You know that. And I promise to do everything I can to make it up to you. Just think about the parent class thing. I think it would be good for the baby, for us, if we're doing this together, even if we're not together, to learn how to be a team for the baby."

"Team Baby, eh?" She chuckled at the idea. He'd totally disarmed her, even when she'd pushed him a bit.

Maybe he was right. Team baby. She knew her sisters would be there if she asked; they always were. But having a mother and a father, together; didn't the baby deserve all the things she never had?

"I'd better skedaddle. Mentioning your sisters reminded me, you don't want them to see me, or we're in a whole other can of worms."

Blair nodded; on that, he was right. She wasn't ready to say yes to parenting classes with him, nor was she ready to tell her sisters where his head was at.

Blake smiled and helped her stand up. "I'll be off, hat on, and I'm parked way down there at The Shack, so no worries. Think about it."

"Okay, thanks for helping with the photos."

She may not be ready to tell her sisters about Blake, but maybe it was time to petition the courts; it was ridiculous to have a PPO against him.

She'd call her lawyer tomorrow.

Thirty

FAYE

Joetta had turned their bi-weekly construction progress meeting into a soap opera, again.

Faye, Blair, and Ali sat, mouths open for a beat, as Joetta, matter-of-fact, almost business-like, explained that her daughters by Banks were actually Kelly Sisters.

"What in the actual—" –" Faye began, but Ali cut her off.

She knew Faye was getting hot, and she was too. Joetta was a chaos demon, that's what was going through Faye's mind. All the work Ali had done to forgive and forge a new family was being blown to smithereens by another lie from Joetta.

"Joetta, Mom, I mean," Ali said before Faye could say any more. "Let me get this straight. Not only are you telling us you were pregnant when Dad kicked you out, but you've been lying to Banks and your twins?"

"Yes. That's the crux of it. I lied. It seemed like the least of the lies."

When she'd come clean about her life, the last time, she had been tentative, remorseful, and afraid of how they'd react. This time, Joetta had barely sat down at the table, ignored the cool drinks Ali had provided, and taken over.

There wasn't even a preamble or a couching of the situation. No "Brace yourself"

No, "I have something big to tell you."

Nothing but her telling them that she was pregnant when she left Toledo, pregnant with two more children of Bruce Kelly. And that was it. Most of all, Faye was angry with Joetta for denying Bruce the opportunity to know Jessie and Jamie.

"When you see Jamie," Joetta continued, "Well, you look just like her, Blair. Anyway. I did it. I thought the only way Banks would want to stay with me was if I were pregnant with his girls. So yes. I lied to him, just like your father lied to you."

Faye struggled to figure out who to be the maddest at. If Bruce hadn't kicked her out, if Joetta had been able to manage her disease earlier...there were a million wrong turns, and now they were here.

And this time, unlike the hospital scene at Didi's bedside, the one who was losing her cool was Faye. She was ready to just give it to Joetta. This was beyond the pale!

"I lied to Banks. I would have told Bruce, but he wouldn't take a single letter or phone call from me. So, I did what I had to do."

Blair shifted in her seat and, as usual, came to Joetta's defense.

"Look, I get it. I am lucky. I have all of you. But if I were doing this alone"—she indicated her growing bump—"I could see maybe grasping at what I could to make a life for my baby."

Faye ignored her and instead charged right in. "Joetta, you are fundamentally incapable of handling a problem without creating five more!"

"I suppose you're right," Joetta said.

Faye could tell she'd hurt her feelings; she felt a little bad. But not that bad. Faye couldn't believe it. Five women, true sisters, who never knew it, thanks to Joetta's convoluted life and logic.

Faye was about to continue berating Joetta out of her own frustration at the woman when Ali cut her off again.

"You're telling this to us now for a reason," Ali said. She was calm. She seemed to be grasping something that Faye didn't.

"Yes. Jessie needs your help."

"We're helping her," Blair said. "I'm doing her socials, and she's been hanging out here to rest, away from the house."

"Yes, I know, and I never even dared to wish for the five of you to be true sisters. And it's happening. But this ask is bigger."

"She's sick, really sick, that's the situation," Ali said.

"Yes." Joetta's all-business mask slipped.

Faye was starting to feel a tinge of remorse for her anger. But only a tinge. Joetta was in a mess she'd created.

"What's the diagnosis?" Blair asked.

"It's called Acute Lymphoblastic Leukemia, ALL for short. It's a blood cancer, and it is moving fast, trying to get my girl." A tear escaped Joetta's eye. She quickly wiped it away.

"What does she need?" Ali asked.

"A bone marrow match. Banks was all about stepping in, and I told him and the girls."

"That had to be hard," Blair said.

"No, this is nothing. You all can hate me forever, Banks can kick me to the curb, I don't care about any of that. I just want her to be okay."

"What does it take? We need to donate blood, or what's the process?" Ali asked.

"Right, we are all on it," Blair said.

"No, not you, honey, you're pregnant, and the donation process is, uh, rugged," Joetta said. "I've been tested and am not a good fit. Jamie would have been a good bet, but she's only got five markers to match."

"Well, I'm in. I'll get tested right away," Ali said.

And then the sisters and Joetta looked at Faye.

Her anger was evaporating as fast as it had materialized. Joetta was right; none of it was as important as getting Jessie whatever she needed.

"Genetically, you three are just as close as her twin, so there's a lot of hope," Joetta said. She seemed to find the strength again, the purpose of blowing up their lives, again.

"I'm in," Faye said. "Where do we go? Just a blood draw or what?"

"Actually, it's in Tampa, and it's a cheek swab, not even a blood draw. But you should know, if it's a match, you need to be on medication that makes you feel really bad for a week. And then they take your blood out, swirl it around, and put it back. It is non-surgical, but it isn't easy. I wished so hard that it was me, that I had the match. But it isn't. And if one of you is, well, I just wanted you to know going in."

"Joetta, we're tough as nails. Bruce made us that way," Ali said.

And she was right; the Kelly Sisters were tough. She thought about Bruce, and how proud he'd have been to know Jamie, one of his girls, was in the military.

So many things Joetta and Bruce had done to break up this bond.

But here they were, ready to give whatever they had to save a sister they just met.

That came from Ali, Faye decided. Ali was the reason they were bonded, and Ali had made sure none of the sisters would hesitate.

Thirty-One

ALI

Her life had been contractors, meetings, worries about bookings, and the random revelations from Joetta. But somehow, Ali was more at peace than she had a right to be.

It was a peace born of fifty years, she'd decided. She was at peace because she realized that life would continue to be tumultuous, even here, by the sea.

She was the match. A perfect match for Jessie. Her newfound little sister needed her strength, all their strength.

She'd met Jessie, what, a month ago, and even in that time she'd gotten smaller, weaker. The little dynamo that they'd first met out on the beach, who was ready to go to battle for their mother, who was ready to throw them all into some sort of scammer's prison, was now allowing them to help her.

Ali was so grateful she could. Everyone who saw them together commented on the fact that they looked more like twins than Jessie and Jamie. Well, twins, if one desperately needed Botox and a facelift, she'd joked. It had made cosmic sense that she'd be the match. She'd felt it before they even took the swab to the lab.

That was the easy part. She was now on Filgrastim, a nasty little drug that had put her stem cell production into high gear. She had to take it the week prior to donation day, and it was effectively kicking her butt.

She could see the parallel beyond looks, between her and Jessie. Her little sister was someone who needed to be in control, to do it all, to not ask for help. Ali saw that and raised a hotel and cottage village to manage along with her own family's dramas.

But the last week had changed that; she was feeling aches, flu-ish, fatigue, and a throbbing headache for extra fun.

She tried to do her normal stiff upper lip routine, tried to meet with the plumbing guy, the HVAC guy, and the appliance guy, but it wasn't working out. She was wiped out. That's when her restaurant guy stepped in.

"Look, your entire family is rallying around Blair and Jessie: you're my project. And I will not be taking notes."

Henry had essentially moved in with her for now at the cottages. Since it was off-season and Blair didn't have it booked for another two weeks, it was the perfect place to lie around, sleep, and just get through until donation day.

She could full well have taken care of herself—she wasn't the one with ALL—but Henry had decided to become her nurse, chef, and bottle washer.

"I have a meeting with the painter; I need to do that."

"I already called Faye," he said, "and she said she's on it. Actually, she's on her way here now. She's consulted with Katie on the right colors, so you don't have to take that meeting."

"Oh, well, seems like you thought of everything." Ali didn't have the energy to really protest.

"How about sitting outside? I've got some juice, and I've pilfered a few snacks from The Seashell Shack."

They were avoiding the Grand Finale; Blair was managing that, much to Ali's secret relief, despite her need to message Blair a complete list of things to do for the event.

"I've got it in our Project Management App now," she'd told her. "All the vendors, all the orders, and quantities based on the number of guests. Since we are at one-third occupancy, the order to Moe's was adjusted accordingly."

Sawyer had also stepped up; his normal cabana boy duties now included pool, laundry, check-ins, and phone answering. He'd been an immense help from the moment he'd decided to make Florida his home. Faye had done such a good job with that kid, er, young man.

Henry had put a few pillows on the two Adirondack chairs. They were so comfy that Ali involuntarily hummed in happiness when she sat down. The salty breeze seemed to clear out her headache, and the cool juice eased her achy joints.

"Okay, so, tomorrow, I've got Joel managing the restaurant, so I'm going to be all in, all day."

The process would take all day, at least four, maybe six hours.

"You have to be kidding me," Ali protested. "I can sit there and chill out, and you can go about your day."

"For a woman preaching to Jessie about accepting help, you sure seem to have a hard time, uh, what's the phrase? Oh yeah, accepting help."

"Oh shh. You're doing a lot already."

"I love you. This is the least of what I want to do for you. And with you." He wagged his eyebrows up and down.

"I'm blushing, or else my fever spiked. And what was it you just said?" She wasn't sure if he realized it.

"I said I love you. Is this shot affecting hearing, too?"

"No, I heard it loud and clear. And I love you too."

Henry leaned over and gave her a kiss on the forehead. Then he sat in the chair next to her and held out his hand.

She put hers in his, and they watched the waterline.

"Look!"

"I see it!"

Two dolphins breached the water and splashed back down.

Ali settled in. Her body was achy, and would be until she was off this medication, but her mind was clear. No grudges, no axes to grind, no lists to manage. She was able to appreciate this very moment in all its sea-salty glory.

Thirty-Two

JESSIE

If there was a low point, she was in it. Jamie couldn't get back; her mother had picked up her kids, and she was so very tired.

Everything she'd tried to build was falling apart.

And now her body was too.

She had been cheerful for her mother. She had put on a brave face for her father.

Even her social media feed, thanks to Blair, conveyed health and happiness.

With her children, she was as honest as she could be, which meant that Mommy is sick, but Mommy will get better.

This wasn't true. It might be true. But it was, but it wasn't guaranteed. The exact match from Ali was good news. Her otherwise healthy lifestyle was also a plus. And the support team she had, well, it was better than anything she could have dreamed.

Her three new sisters had quickly become nearly as close to her as Jamie. Well, as close as they could be on short notice.

The diagnosis was a shortcut, she realized. She didn't have the time to hold back on her affection for the people who were stepping up. For the first time in her adult life, she wasn't in control. She had zero control, actually.

The Sea Turtle had become her happy place. She watched the birds there. She watched families. She even watched her two little girls learn how to boogie board with Sawyer. Maybe, when this was all over, she'd learn too.

She prayed this would be over, but the worst was yet to come. Chemo would break down her defective immune system, her bad blood, and Ali's would replace it.

But the breakdown would be a bear. She watched the girls play. She was about to call for someone to reapply sunscreen when another beach chair plopped down beside her.

She expected Ali, Faye, or even Blair, though it was getting harder for the pregnant Blair to get back out of the beach chair.

Jessie turned to look, and there was Landon. He'd called, he'd tried to set up a time, he'd done a lot to connect. But she didn't have the energy for her failing marriage right now.

He'd have to hate her on his own with no help from her. She was over whatever issues she'd had with him. She'd failed at that, too, the good wife thing. And now there was nothing left but the formal separation. Was that why he was here? To get her to sign something?

She'd also ignored calls from the mediator. Jessie's focus was on her treatment and her girls. Landon's problems would have to be Landon's.

"I must be dying."

"You're not."

"Why else would you be here, on the beach, in the middle of a workday?"

"I took a leave of absence. We're going to be spending a lot more time together. Lucky you."

"What are you talking about? Don't change your social life on my account. Last I heard, I was stifling your joy—uh, what was it?

Hen pecking the daylights out of you or some such." She meant for her words to be biting, but they came out weak. Sad. That's what she was now.

"Boss me all you want," Landon said. She laughed at that.

"Well, somehow I've lost the will to give a crap about laundry and dishwasher loading deficits."

"I do perfectly good laundry, I stand by that."

"Okay, I surrender."

"That's the absolute last thing you're going to do. You're going to fight like hell, you hear me?"

"I don't know if I can." She felt her lip quiver. The fear was under the surface and threatening to come out.

"You can, but you can also be afraid. I can take it. I can take all of it."

"I've had to give them a different face," she pointed out to the kids.

"Oh, I know, and your mother will not tolerate any talk of you being scared. But I know you are, and it's okay. I'm here. Lay it on me."

"What does that mean, you're here? Like now? Or ten minutes from now? Or tomorrow?"

"It means forever. I shouldn't have left. I am sorry. I'll never stop trying to make it up to you. Like I said. I'd even consider loading the dishwasher your way and reading the laundry tags. That's how serious I am."

She laughed again, and then something shifted. She wanted to cry, but the girls were on the beach, and she didn't want to scare them.

"It's okay, they're totally immersed in surfer boy's lessons." He got out of the chair and hunched over to her. "Move over, lard butt. We can share."

Landon pulled her up, sat down, and plopped her on his lap. It was comforting, familiar, and a huge relief. Whatever their problems were, it was nothing in comparison to what she was now dealing with.

They sat there together for a while. She cried, and then pulled herself together.

"Now, while you comport yourself, I'm going to go nag the children for reapplication of sunscreen."

"Wait, I'm the one who nags. You're the fun one. How in the world will the kids react to that?"

"They'll have to get used to it. I've decided to become a grade A type A dad until you're back in action."

And from that moment forward, she had her partner back. Landon was there for all of it. For every treatment, school pick-ups, tough discussions with the doctors, and a load of laundry.

Thirty-Three

BLAIR

She'd promised Blake she'd remove the PPO, and she was going to do it.

The county clerk's office was lit with fluorescent lights that buzzed in a way that seemed designed to give her a migraine.

She sat on a hard plastic chair that was not designed for a woman who was six months pregnant. A woman behind a glass partition was typing something, slowly, and then she answered a phone, and then she called across the cubicle farm to someone else.

Finally, she called Blair's name.

Blair walked up to the window.

"You're dismissing the motion entirely?" asked the clerk, not looking up. Her voice was flat, bored, stripped of judgment. She'd likely seen just about everything from behind that plexiglass.

"Yes," Blair said. Her voice sounded thin in the high-ceilinged room. She cleared her throat and sat up straighter. "Yes. We've...resolved the issues."

The clerk stopped typing. She looked over her glasses. "This is a Personal Protection Order, ma'am. It was granted because of a finding of immediate danger. You understand that by dismissing this, the respondent can contact you, come to your home, and approach you in public?"

"I know what it means," Blair said, a little sharper than she intended. She tried to soften her tone. "There was a misunderstanding. We're better. He's better. Truly."

She didn't explain her fear of going through this pregnancy alone. Blair was doing the unselfish thing here, she reasoned. She was giving her baby a chance at two parents, at all the best in life. Even if Blake hadn't started out as the best boyfriend, he'd been growing into being a good dad.

People could change. Her own family was evidence of that. It was constant growth and change.

"I need you to sign here, here, and initial here," The clerk slid a clipboard under the glass.

Blair took the pen. It felt heavy. The ink was black and permanent. She looked at the signature line. *Petitioner: Blair Kelly.*

Blair signed the paper. The scratch of the pen was loud. With that ink, she dissolved the invisible wall the state had built around her. She was accessible again. She was open.

"Alright," Doris said, stamping the document with a heavy *thud* that made Blair flinch. "It'll be processed by the end of the day. The Sheriff's department will serve him notice that the order is vacated."

"Thank you."

Blair walked out of the courthouse into the blinding afternoon sun. She fished her phone out of her bag.

She texted Blake: *It's all set.*

She watched the three dots. Blake was responding.

You won't regret this. We're on the way to the happiest little family!

She typed back: *Don't get ahead of yourself, we're going to Lamaze classes, that's all this is.*

Blair was meeting Faye at the baby store. She tried to stop thinking about what she'd just done. It was no big deal, really, and it made sense.

But she also didn't feel ready to tell anyone yet—Faye, or Ford, or anyone.

Faye greeted her at Target.

"Okay, so it's infant car seat fun!" Faye was legitimately hopping up and down with glee over their shopping list.

Blair didn't want to get too much; she didn't want a shower, she just wanted to be calm, healthy, and responsible. That's what this was with Blake, the responsible thing to do.

But she couldn't stop her sisters from wanting to get all the baby things, as they said. Ali had decided that the Blueberry Bungalo was hers for now. She knew this was a temporary solution; they'd need to get it rented. But she also didn't want to pay for an apartment. They were all on a shoestring while The Sea Turtle rentals slowly added up. They weren't fully booked, and they wouldn't be until the inn was done.

Still, Faye was making good cash, she said, with the flowers, and she was going to spend it on her niece.

"The first time we put Sawyer in his car seat, it was a total disaster. He was tiny, and the seat wasn't right. Leave it to Budd to screw that up. We go driving down Douglas Road, and it pops open. I freaked."

"Yikes, yeah, I do not want that."

They settled in on a car seat for infants that could pop out of the base and into a stroller or into a grocery cart. It looked like something out of Star Trek.

"This is great, no need for an extra carrier this way," Faye explained. Blair was getting a little tired, she had to admit. From the hospital to the courthouse to this shopping, she'd probably overbooked her day. Her phone buzzed.

It was Blake.

Text me the class schedule, ASAP, I'm so excited.

"Anything wrong? Ali? Jessie? Joetta reveals she has three more siblings she left at a circus."

Blair laughed. Faye was having a harder time than Ali over the lying about the twins. But Ali's selflessness had helped them all realize the most important thing was getting Jessie healthy, not busting Joetta's chops about the past. If they were lucky and Jessie's body accepted the transplant and survived all the chemo, they'd have a lot of time to bust Joetta's chops over the lies she had told.

So many lies. Blair realized she had a talent too, for lying too. And she did it with ease in the car seat aisle.

"Nope, all is well, just a weather alert. Record heat tomorrow."

"Ah, Florida. Let's make it a beach day then." Faye wandered over to the baby clothes and was transfixed by the onesies.

Blair looked at her phone. She texted the class schedule to Blake and let him know she'd meet him there.

Thirty-Four

JESSIE

She was in the hospital for a few days before the donation. She was antsy, bored, scared, and determined, all rolled up into one person.

Her pretty pregnant sister was there for a visit. She welcomed the chance to talk about anything but cancer.

"Maybe a little distraction would be welcome?"

Blair had been disinfected from head to toe, her computer wiped down, and her temperature taken. Jessie was incredibly vulnerable to infection, and for a few days she'd been in the hospital, essentially, in a bubble.

Blair and Jessie were the closest in age. Jessie thought about how little Blair had to have been when their mother left. A baby still. And for all intents and purposes, Jessie was a baby now, when it came to her immune system.

It seemed to Jessie that Blair had the closest bond with Joetta. Maybe she hadn't had any bad memories with her, or no memories at all.

Whatever the reason, Jessie had easily bonded with Blair. Ali was like the big sister angel saint type, Faye, a firecracker with a similar disposition to Jamie, but Blair, well, they just meshed.

"A distraction would be nice," Jessie said.

And Blair, now very pregnant, waddled in. For a brief second, Jessie thought about her pregnancies. She'd never affirmatively decided not to have more; Landon sort of wanted a third. But now that was out of the question. Her body was having enough trouble just staying alive, much less growing a baby.

She wasn't sad about not having more, but it was easy to compare, seeing Blair, about to start this journey.

"How are you feeling?"

"I'm feeling tired, but honestly, grateful."

Her small, quiet, fancy, and stilted family had turned big, brash, and colorful, almost overnight. Her illness was scary, but it showed her so many things that weren't. For one, that Ali is an absolute rock star, enduring the pain of the bone marrow transplant for her. A woman she'd just met. Ali should resent her. Right? Ali lost her mother, and Jessie and Jamie gained her.

But it was none of their faults, and miraculously, Ali seemed the most evolved, the most healed.

Jessie didn't really know Faye yet, but wanted to. Her new sister was sending her pictures of flowers since she couldn't have flowers in the room, too much of a risk of some spore attacking her infant's immune system.

"We're grateful it all went well," Blair said now. "We just got you. We've got a lot of catching up to do."

"Honestly, I can't wait for you all to meet Jamie. I think she's the most like Faye of the three of you."

"Any word on that?"

"No, she said she's trying to get here. I will be so happy when she does."

"Well, let me pinch hit. The three of us are practically the same age."

"Very true. I want to thank you for digging in and keeping my socials going. I think not a soul knows I'm not actually posting in real time."

Blair had been reposting, looking at her analytics to see which videos to repurpose, and even answering brand deal questions. Though those were drying up; her meltdown took care of that.

"So that's what I want to show you." Blair pulled her laptop out and flipped it open.

Jessie scootched up in the bed, and Blair propped the computer on her food tray.

"Have you looked at the comments since you had your meltdown?"

"I looked at them that day, and they were awful, and then all this. The doctor doesn't want me to be stressed, so I just pretended it didn't happen. Denial, they call it."

"I get it. But I have looked at the comments on your post, your accidental live, and on the one the car place customer posted."

"Ugh, this is not my favorite topic."

"I think it should be."

"All those years of building a brand and poof."

"No, not poof. Let me give you the Cliff's Notes. People LOVE the real you."

"Right, give me a break. They love filters and glass skin and white carpet."

"Actually, Jodie from Cleveland says she relates to this so much. Carrie in Hoboken says she is you and you are her. Janice in Idaho says, and I quote, 'Hells yeah.'"

"Are these a few among all the crappy ones?"

"No, these are the overwhelming majority of comments. Women. Stressed-out women. Moms. They love this. They love you."

Jessie was shocked to say the least.

All that time trying to be perfect, and the best engagement she'd had in years was her dropping her basket in the middle of a car repair shop!?

"Well, unfortunately, losing my crap is not something I want to repeat, and it's hard to monetize, unless maybe Lorazepam sponsors me?"

They both laughed at that.

"I think you can go in this direction," Blair said. "In fact, it could be the best direction. The numbers show you were shrinking on views, engagement, and native discovery. Like, it was pretty dire."

"I know. I was going to have to get a job, right?"

"Well, now, you see this hockey stick? It's all the things; you've gained over half-million new followers on all your platforms. And just about every day you average 10K more."

"You're kidding me."

"I am serious. And what that says to me is, no, you don't freak out on the socials as a job, but maybe there's a real chance for you to relaunch a different kind of channel."

"What kind? The 'Jessie is a Complete Mess' podcast and YouTube." She was completely joking.

"Exactly that kind."

Jessie's mind turned the idea over and over. "I have to think."

"I know, and you're supposed to rest. I just thought maybe you'd like some good news and maybe you'd like to think of something other than all this." Blair pointed to the monitors beside her bed.

"Thank you, Blair, for all you've done. And for maybe opening a window?"

"You're welcome. Now, if I don't let you rest, then Joetta will kick my butt. She's little, but dang, she's ferocious."

"Yeah, she once crawled on her hands and knees into the kitchen to spy on my boyfriend and me to make sure I wasn't, well, you know."

"I believe it. And were you?"

"Of course not, I'm Miss Perfect."

"I'd say you're messy, and we love it."

$$Thirty-Five$$

JOETTA

All of the energy, attention, and emotion that Joetta and Banks had in them was directed at Jessie. They had never faced this kind of challenge. Joetta could see that Jessie didn't want them to worry, that their daughter, true to form, wanted to do it all on her own. But slowly she watched as Ali, Faye, and Blair folded themselves into Jessie's life. It was fast, but it was gentle. It gave her hope that she could continue to be a part of all of her girls' lives.

She had stayed at The Sea Turtle until one day, well, Banks and Joetta had gotten their wires crossed. Both of them showed up at the dance recital rehearsal to pick up their little granddaughter, Joy.

"Oh, I thought that was me. I thought it was me," said Joetta.

Banks said, "It was, but I feel like maybe it's time—time for us to have a talk."

So while little Joy practiced her sashay and sparkle fingers, the two of them sat in the back of the rehearsal space, far away from any dance moms.

"Well, you know it all now."

"I do."

"Did you ever suspect?"

"I did."

"Why didn't you ever say anything?"

"Because I loved you. And you also met the girls. They're part of you. You know they're part of you, too," she said.

Banks nodded. "They are. I don't need any DNA test or any of the specifics to know they're my girls. Question is, are you still—"

Joetta couldn't believe what she was hearing. "I don't know. I mean, of course. But I just thought you maybe wouldn't be able to forgive me."

"Well, it's been a process, as the kids say. At first, I just didn't want to deal with it—or you. It felt like you were using me all this time."

"That's not the case. I mean, when I saw you back then, I realized what a fool I looked like, but you can't blame me too much for that. When I left Florida, I was sixteen years old. So stupid."

"I don't blame you for that. I was hurt then, but I'll never forget seeing you again. I knew that my heart would only be yours."

Joetta started to cry, but she didn't want to show him. She couldn't believe how it felt to hear that there was still a place in his heart for her. "But then I lied about the girls, too."

"You know you did. But instead of being forced or having me find out by taking a blood test, you stepped up. I think that says something."

"Yeah? What does it say?"

"It says maybe you're done with lies."

"Yeah. I am done with lies. That's why I moved out. I couldn't believe that everything was okay with us when you were clearly, well, so distant."

"Yeah, I did need some time. But I'm ready, if you're ready, to start again."

He put his hand down. She put her hand in his. He rested their clasped hands on his knee.

"We have to get this sorted out," he said, "so that we can give Jessie everything that she needs."

"Agreed."

"Now what about—what about your other three?"

"I guess I have to start coming to the Grand Finale."

"I guess you do. But I think you need to move back home."

"Well, okay. The beach is pretty nice," she laughed.

"Look, I haven't been able to find my golf ball tie since you left. If nothing else, you've got to help me find it."

They had been together for so long. She knew exactly where it was, but she knew exactly why he couldn't see it.

Banks proved one more time that he was the best man she ever knew.

Thirty-Six

JESSIE

The bag of stem cells didn't seem to have magical properties. She was thinking it ought to be like a scene out of Harry Potter. Wasn't this a magical elixir set to save her life? But it wasn't glowing or golden; it was just a small, translucent pouch filled with a pinkish-orange fluid.

Jessie lay propped up in her hospital bed, the sterile sheets crisp against her legs. The room hummed with the quiet, rhythmic beeping of monitors.

"Here we go, sweetie," the nurse, a kind woman named Ellen with gentle hands and bright blue scrubs, said softly. She spiked the bag and hung it on the IV pole next to a saline drip. "Happy Birthday."

In the transplant ward, Day Zero was the day you were born again. It was the day your immune system, scorched by chemotherapy, was replaced with a new one. This one courtesy of Ali.

"It might smell a little like creamed corn," Ellen warned, adjusting the drip. "That's just the preservative."

"Creamed corn," Jessie whispered. "My favorite."

As the fluid began to travel down the clear tubing, Jessie closed her eyes. She felt a coldness in her chest as the chilled cells entered her central line. *Grow,* she told the cells. *Please, just grow.*

She thought of Ali. Of all her sisters. She was grateful for every single one of them. Four of them. They did all they could. Now it was up to her.

An hour later, the bag was empty. The "transplant" was over. No trumpets or TA DA! Just an empty bag.

There was a soft knock on the glass door.

"Come in," Jessie rasped.

The heavy door slid open, and suddenly, the sterile room was filled with color. Landon walked in first, his eyes crinkling at the corners above his mask. He was holding a massive bouquet of balloons—silver stars and pink hearts. Behind him, her mother, Joetta, carried a tray of store-bought and sealed cupcakes, in accordance with the strict rules Jessie had been under for quite a while.

"You okay, babe?" Landon asked, his voice muffled by the mask but thick with emotion.

"I'm a work in progress," Jessie said, reaching out a hand.

Landon crossed the room in two strides and took her hand. His grip was warm and solid. He looked steady. He was steady. He had turned into the man he was meant to be. And her days of flipping out over stupid things, well, they were gone, just like the animosity they'd held onto before all this happened.

"You did well, Jess," he whispered, squeezing her fingers. "I'm so proud of you."

Joetta set the cupcakes down on the rolling table and bustled over, her eyes shining. "Well? Do you feel different?"

Jessie laughed. "I just feel... hopeful."

"Hopeful is good," Joetta said firmly. She looked around the room for something to straighten and settled on smoothing the bed sheets. "Hopeful is everything."

Landon leaned down and kissed her forehead, right above the

mask line. "The kids made you a card. It's the size of a billboard. I left it with the nurses at the station to sanitize."

"They drew you as Dolly Parton," Joetta added. "They're on a Dolly Parton kick for some reason."

Jessie looked at them—her husband, her mother. She thought of all the people who had held her up.

She looked at the empty bag hanging on the pole. The cells were inside her now. Ali's cells. Ali was the strongest person she'd ever met, next to Jamie. And now both of them were forever a part of her.

She knew that would be enough.

Thirty-Seven

JESSIE

Blair had created anticipation; she called it "Operation Relaunch."

It was a good name considering just about every part of Jessie's life was a relaunch. She was relaunching herself as a wife, as a mother, and even down to her blood. It was all new.

She was on day one-hundred. Day zero, Ali's transplant donation got to work; over two months later, Dr. Walls was calling her the "Gold Standard" patient. She was doing everything perfectly, except this time it wasn't perfect hair, house, makeup, and outfits. No, this time it was perfect hydration, nutrition, sleep, and stress management.

And her family, Landon, June, and Joy, were her self-care. Landon was handling anything school-related since an elementary school was a literal Petrie dish of possible infections. Ali, Faye, and Blair were pinch-hitting on everything and anything. And in a stress reliever of epic proportions, her parents were acting normal! Well, normal-ish. Mom was back at the house with Dad, and Dad was looking at Mom like the sun rose and set around her. Whatever they had to work out with Mom's lies, they were doing without burdening Jessie and Jamie. A child, no matter how old, should never have to deal with their parents' marital issues.

Jamie was the one disappointing spot. She still hadn't made it home. A lot of calls and care packages, but she hadn't been able to get away. That stung. But Jessie knew she wouldn't be holding a grudge. If something was toxic, including her own emotions, she let it go. She was determined that she would be the best possible host for the gift that Ali had freely and immediately given her.

Blair had strategized with her on a new direction for her business. And had helped coach her that it was a business. Separating her work and her home, but also being honest about what was working for her business, was invigorating. They'd come up with a plan. Every day for the last two weeks, Blair created a new graphic that hinted at her new direction. People could even sign up for a newsletter for exclusive insider access. Blair had helped her structure the whole thing.

And finally, it was time.

She watched the countdown. It would be live, but she didn't have a lick of makeup on. Instead of her slicked-back blonde pony, her hair, what she had of it, was hidden under a scarf. It was an adorable scarf, if she did say so herself, but it was one she'd bought. There were no hauls, there was also no perfect persona. It was just Jessie in her kitchen, which was by all accounts an unruly mess.

As the countdown ended—three, two, one —she looked at the camera standing on the tripod perched on her not-so-pristine countertop, and she began.

"Hi. I know it's been a while. But I hit a bad patch. A major one. And maybe you've noticed I've had some changes here. I was very sick, and I am still not out of the woods, but I'm doing great."

She explained her diagnosis briefly, and she explained that she had just recently had a transplant.

"It has been three months since my transplant, and things are going great, but for all intents and purposes, I'm a baby. I'm getting vaccines again in a year. I'm trying not to get any sort of cold or flu, so my life is a little bit different—well, a lot different—than the last time I went live on this channel.

"The last time I went live on this channel, you saw me, as my mother calls it, drop my basket. I was overstressed, trying to be perfect, and it turns out I was really sick too. Well, that leads me to the changes.

"I've gotten so many messages from so many of you in the exact same boat. You're stressed out, overworked, and under pressure to have everything just perfect. And I'm telling you, nothing was perfect. So I'm relaunching. As you've seen over the last few days, my channel has been renamed, and what you're going to see from me is different.

"I'm going to show you what it's really like to be a mom of two, to be a wife, and try to run my business — because this is my business. What I show you will be the things that I actually use and buy myself. There will be no hauls or freebies. If I use it and I like it, I'll tell you about it. If I use it and I don't like it, you'll hear that too. You'll also see behind the scenes. If it takes me all day to make a lasagna noodle or maybe pretend to make it, you'll see that too. I want to put content out into the world that lets all women know what it's really like to do your best, succeed sometimes, and fail a lot too.

"I'm done with perfect hair. Well, right now I don't have hardly any hair at all. And I won't be bothering with a perfect makeup job. Actually, right now my skin is kind of sensitive, so you're looking at my face with zero makeup. Lip gloss, and that's it. That's something I never would've done before.

"I have learned a lot about what is really important to me. So here it is. I want to be a great mom, a good wife, and a relatable leader in this community that we've built.

"So, if this video—this live—winds up making any money, all of it that I earn I'm going to show you, and it will be donated to the ALL Foundation, which has helped me immensely over the past six months navigate a whole new world.

"Now onto my content. So this thing was sent to me because it's supposed to get rid of wrinkles."

She held up a red, scary-looking mask.

"Let me tell you something—it doesn't."

Then she got really close to the camera and showed her little furrow.

"Yeah, that's right. No more Botox for this girl. It's dangerous for me, so you're going to see a lot of scowling and a lot of wrinkles. But let me tell you, most of my wrinkles these days come from smiling. I hope that I can make you smile too.

"And the name of the channel, just so you know, is Jessie's Messy. So welcome to Jessie's Messy. I hope you stick with me. If you want real talk, real bargains, real good stuff for your life with a heaping helping of disaster, I think I might be the channel for you."

She was about to click the button to end the live. But instead, she put her hand up the scarf and slid it off. She gently rubbed the downy fur on her mostly bald head. She gave a little wink and then she clicked the button to end the live.

Thirty-Eight

JAMIE

It was called the Grand Finale. Her mom and Jessie had been going on and on about it. She hadn't been home in two years, and when she went to surprise her mom, no one was home. Same with Jessie's house. That's when she remembered the Grand Finale.

So she paid the Uber guy extra to drive her out to Haven Beach. The stifling traffic of Tampa slowly morphed into something else. As he drove over the bridge to the islands, something started to shift in her.

"Do you mind if I open a window?"

"No problem," he answered, "anything for our military. Appreciate your service so much."

Jamie nodded. She was still in her fatigues from her travels. Not exactly beachwear. But she did have a bag; there was a suit in there somewhere.

The salty air put a smile on her face. It was different here, she remembered. They so rarely came out here when she was growing up. She supposed it was a way for Mom to distance herself from her wild youth. Who knew Joetta was ever wild? I guess if your mom was wild, you sort of don't want to know.

Jessie had been fully pulled into the Kelly Sisters' coven, or whatever they were. It sparked a little FOMO in her, she had to admit. It was supposed to be Jessie and Jamie versus the world. But when Jessie needed her, she couldn't get here. That led to so much of what was happening right now. Jamie blocked it out. She didn't want to think about how and why she was sitting in this Uber headed to the aptly named Haven Beach.

They pulled into the parking lot of The Sea Turtle. Jamie was shocked. She and her sister had rejected the offer to be part owners, but now, looking at the place, she second-guessed that. It was a cute-as-heck retro hotel and a village of cottages.

Wow.

If it wasn't booked yet it was only because the world didn't know about it. She hoisted her bag onto her shoulder and added a tip in her app for the driver. The warm sun went a long way toward pushing out the chill in her heart. She had been keeping everything locked up tight. She had to keep doing that. Her sister didn't need to be burdened. Jessie needed to be lifted up. The idea that she could have lost Jessie was unthinkable.

Jamie walked down a sandy path through the colorful cottage village. There were charming decks on each one, beach towels swayed on the rails, and palm trees shaded her walk towards the beach. She crouched behind a lush, nearly wild, thicket of sea grape. Jamie wasn't quite ready to dive into the sea of people.

They all look so happy!

A woman who looked exactly like her mother and Jessie walked hand in hand with a handsome silver fox that was a ringer for Timothy Olyphant. Ah, and that must be Ali, she thought. She owed Ali so much. Ali's boyfriend slid something on her finger. They thought they were unobserved, no doubt. Jamie watched as Ali kissed the man.

Another group were enjoying a beach volleyball game. A

twenty-something who looked straight out of a California surfer ad was spiking a ball and warning, "MOM! This one's on you!" The woman dove for it and likely just took a mouthful of sand! A buff-looking dude helped her up. This must be Faye; she'd seen pictures of them all on their floral Instagram.

And then another woman walked, or rather waddled over, hand in hand with a guy that did not look like he ought to be on the beach. He wore a polo shirt and madras shorts, but his hair was too perfect, his arm possessive over the woman. And dang, if she wasn't pregnant, this woman was like looking in a mirror. Blair. While everyone hugged Blair and offered to help her navigate into a beach chair, the man was awkward. There seemed to be less enthusiasm for seeing him.

Wonder what the story there was?

Jamie realized that Mom must have known that anyone who would see Blair would know she was related. Jamie and Blair were twins; in the face, at least!

These strangers were her sisters. This just blew her mind. Not her half-sisters, her full-blood sisters. She'd gone from one to four in the blink of an eye. This was almost too much to process. Jessie had opened her heart to them already. Jamie didn't know how to do that. They were strangers.

And then she scanned the chairs, lined up in a row. Mom, Dad, Aunt Didi, and Jorge sat with their shoes kicked off and a fruity drink in hand. They laughed at the antics playing out in front of them of June and Joy, performing some sort of elaborate Haven Beach Dance.

The girls are so big!

Jamie cursed herself for the time she'd missed. And she cried. She didn't mean to, but she felt a hot tear on her cheek. Time moved so fast when you were away. She'd been away so long.

"Hey, you really shouldn't be spying on these nice people."

And there, right next to her, behind the sea grape cover, was

Jessie. Covered from head to toe, looking like an adorable little mummy more than a beach bunny.

"Sissy!"

Jessie nearly knocked the wind out of Jamie with the squeeze she gave her. Jamie was horrified at the delicate feel of Jessie in her arms. Her sister was still in this fight. Jamie could feel it. See it.

"You're looking like a baby bird," Jamie said.

"I kind of am one, all downy hair and such."

"How are you feeling?"

"So much better now that you're here. I thought you couldn't get away?"

"Yeah, well, here I am. And I'm here for a while, to help get you back to fighting weight."

"So you can fight with me?"

"Exactly." She squeezed Jessie one more time, and over her shoulder was Landon; he gave her a little wave.

"All good with the Mister, I see."

"All good with so much. Now that you're here, all good with everything! Come on, Mom and Aunt Didi are going to flip out to see you!"

Jessie took her hand and started to drag her forward into the family, onto the beach, and thankfully away from her very recent past. Which she needed to forget.

"Welcome to the Grand Finale," Jessie whispered.

Her family saw her, and as Jessie predicted, flipped. Her mother and aunt popped out of their beach chairs with the agility of much younger women.

Jamie looked out to the horizon to glimpse the real star of the show. A gorgeous fireball turned the sky every shade of orange you could imagine. It sank into the ocean. An ocean, she hoped, would be enough distance between her and what had happened.

Jamie accepted hundreds of hugs and kisses on this perfect stretch of Haven Beach.

The story of the Kelly Sisters continues in Gulfside Sunset
Sign up for Rebecca Regnier's Newsletter to get an exclusive first look at Gulfside Sunset.

Also by Rebecca Regnier

Summer Cottage Novels

- Sandbar Sisters
- Sandbar Season
- Sandbar Summer
- Sandbar Storm
- Sandbar Sunrise

Haven Beach Beachy Women's Fiction Series

- Gulfside Girls
- Gulfside Inn
- Gulfside Secret
- Gulfside Wish
- Gulfside Sunset

About the Author

Rebecca Regnier is an award-winning newspaper columnist, tv host, and former television news anchor. She lives in Michigan with her family and handsome dog. For all the latest from the beach and an exclusive bonus scene sign up for her newsletter or follow her on one of her socials. She loves to share laughs with her readers!

tiktok.com/@rebeccaregnier

facebook.com/rlregnier

instagram.com/rebeccaregnier

youtube.com/@RebeccaRegnierTV